Houston Sadler ... **A billionaire. An**... **to getting exactly what he wanted.**

Gabrielle had seen the love in Houston's eyes when he looked at Lucas, and that love might blind him to the fact that this was the child she'd planned and carried. This was *her* baby.

He showed her to her room, and it was even larger than she'd expected. There was even a crib and changing table.

"You're exhausted," Houston commented.

And as if it was the most normal and routine thing in the world, he took Lucas from her arms and carried him to the crib. He didn't lay the baby down right away, but instead kissed his cheek and smiled at him.

Gabrielle could see it then—the strong resemblance. It was uncanny and unnerving just how much Lucas looked like his father. He was indeed a Sadler.

That didn't do much to steady her nerves.

DELORES FOSSEN

THE MOMMY MYSTERY

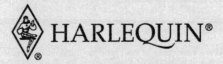

HARLEQUIN®

TORONTO • NEW YORK • LONDON
AMSTERDAM • PARIS • SYDNEY • HAMBURG
STOCKHOLM • ATHENS • TOKYO • MILAN • MADRID
PRAGUE • WARSAW • BUDAPEST • AUCKLAND

Recycling programs
for this product may
not exist in your area.

ISBN-13: 978-0-373-69484-6

THE MOMMY MYSTERY

Copyright © 2010 by Delores Fossen

Printed in U.S.A.

ABOUT THE AUTHOR

Imagine a family tree that includes Texas cowboys, Choctaw and Cherokee Indians, a Louisiana pirate and a Scottish rebel who battled side by side with William Wallace. With ancestors like that, it's easy to understand why Texas author and former air force captain Delores Fossen feels as if she were genetically predisposed to writing romances. Along the way to fulfilling her DNA destiny, Delores married an air force top gun who just happens to be of Viking descent. With all those romantic bases covered, she doesn't have to look too far for inspiration.

Books by Delores Fossen

CAST OF CHARACTERS

Houston Sadler—The last thing this billionaire rancher expects is to hear that his old nemesis, Gabrielle Markham, has given birth to his son. Even though Houston hasn't counted on fatherhood in his immediate future, he wants to claim his child. First, though, he must deal with the feelings he has for the baby's mother and the danger she brings right to his doorstep.

Gabrielle Markham—When this single mom applied for a donor embryo, she had no idea she'd be giving birth to Houston's son, and she certainly hadn't counted on falling hard for a man she once considered her enemy.

Lucas—The newborn at the center of the controversy. His unexpected birth places both his father and mother in grave danger.

Jay Markham—Gabrielle's brother. He has an ax to grind with Houston, and he might be willing to involve Gabrielle and Lucas to get revenge.

Mack Sadler—Houston's father, who would do anything to ensure there's a Sadler heir.

Dale Burnett—The foreman at the Sadler Ranch. He's used to covering up Mack's interference, but this time he might have gone too far.

Harlan Cordell—He lent Jay Markham a lot of money and he plans to be repaid in full, even if that means going after Gabrielle and her newborn.

Salvador Franks—Head of the clinic where Gabrielle got the donor embryo. Is Franks guilty of tricking Gabrielle into surrogacy so Mack Sadler can have the heir he's always wanted?

Chapter One

Blue Springs Ranch, Texas

Houston Sadler climbed down from his horse, eased off his Stetson and smacked it against his jeans to get rid of some of the dust he'd accumulated on his ride. Bear, his buckskin gelding, snorted in protest, and Houston led the horse into the stables so he could brush him down.

Neither of them got far.

"Don't move," someone said.

Houston didn't have time to move, or think, before he felt the barrel of a gun jam against his back.

"Lift your hands so I can see them," the gunman added. Or rather the gun*woman,* because that was a female's voice.

Now the question was, what the hell did she want?

"If you're after money, there's none in the stables, and I don't have my wallet with me," Houston let her know.

He lifted his hands, releasing Bear's reins so the gelding would get out of the way. He damn sure didn't want his horse to get hurt when he took down this would-be robber. And there were no ifs, ands or buts about it, he was going to take her down. No one got away with pulling a gun on him.

"I'm not after your money," she spat out, as if he'd insulted her. Her voice was clogged and hoarse, and he thought he heard her sniffle.

"Are you thinking about kidnapping me?" he asked, trying another tack.

If so, she wouldn't get far, because his ranch hands were all over the place. In fact, one could and probably would come into the stables at any moment. All of Houston's men knew his schedule and knew he'd be at the tail end of his daily ride. At least one would likely come in and offer to groom Bear.

"I'm not here to kidnap you." Her voice was little more than a whisper now, and she didn't add anything else to tell him her intentions.

So, if this wasn't about money, then it was about love or revenge. But those were the likely reasons *if* he was dealing with a semisane person. He could rule out love, since he hadn't had more than a basic, no-strings-attached sexual relationship with a woman since his wife died three years ago.

That left revenge.

And if that was the case, then she probably intended to kill him. Or at least try.

"Do I know you?" he asked. Houston angled his head just slightly and looked over his shoulder. Then he cursed.

Oh, yeah. He knew her.

"Gabrielle Markham," Houston grumbled, and turned to face her.

He also dropped his hands. His mouth dropped open,

too. She was the last person he expected to see in his stables with a gun on him.

But he rethought that.

The last time they'd crossed paths was…what?…a year ago? Maybe longer. She'd been dressed in a dove-gray business suit in the Bexar County courthouse, where she'd tried to sue his jeans off on behalf of her client, who also happened to be her brother, Jay.

She'd lost the case. Or rather, it'd been dismissed for lack of evidence.

Which meant Houston was back to the revenge motive, even though this was a pretty extreme measure for someone sour over losing a legal battle. People lost legal battles to him all the time.

Houston stared at her, trying to make sense of this situation and her. She certainly wasn't wearing a business suit today. Khaki pants and a pale pink shirt that was bulky and loose. She was also pale, no makeup, and the whites of her brown eyes were red.

She'd been crying, all right.

Her short, blond hair was spiky and uncombed, and it didn't look as if she'd done it to make a fashion statement. The cool October breeze rustled through it, messing it up even more than it already was.

"What happened?" Houston wasn't just alarmed now, he was concerned. Not so much for the woman who was holding him at gunpoint, but for whatever had driven her to come out to the Blue Springs ranch and commit a felony.

Gabrielle cleared her throat. "You tell me what happened. I want answers, and I want them now."

He gave her a flat look. "You took the words right

out of my mouth. Since I'm the one at gunpoint, I think I deserve an answer or two."

Those teary brown eyes narrowed. "Don't play games with me, Houston Sadler. You might have half the money in Texas, but I won't let you get away with this. Why did you do it? *Why?*"

Houston shrugged and tried to stay calm. Hard to do with that gun on him. "Because your brother was wrong to try to sue me, that's why. He was fired for a legitimate reason. Because he abused one of the cutting mares. Jay's damn lucky I didn't go after him the way he did that mare. Instead of beating him senseless, I fired his sorry butt. There was no wrongful dismissal involved. End of story."

Gabrielle shook her head. "This doesn't have anything to do with my brother." She paused, blinked. "Does it? Did you do this to get back at him by using me?"

Houston huffed. He was tired of these nonsense questions and having a Saturday-night special aimed at him.

He made sure Bear was out of the way first. The gelding was. So he lowered his head and dove right at Gabrielle. He didn't hit her with his full weight, and cursed himself for being a gentleman at a time like this.

They landed hard, against the stable wall, and her hand smacked right into his groin. She probably hadn't planned to do that, but it worked. Houston saw stars and growled in pain. He also grabbed her hands, pinning them to the wall so she couldn't fire that gun.

Gabrielle fought back. No surprise there. Houston hadn't expected her to give up without a struggle.

He maneuvered his body so that he held her in place.

It wasn't that hard to do. She was five-four, if that, and her feeble attempts to hit him landed like weak thuds on his chest. She was what his father would have called a *"pretty little thing."* Houston figured he could add "desperate" to that particular description.

"Now, tell me why you're here," he insisted. "And I'm not giving you another chance. Talk now, or I yell for my ranch foreman. He'll come running, then call the sheriff, who'll haul your butt off to jail. Got that?"

Her breath gusted against his face, and she continued to glare at him before she finally started to relax. When she nodded, Houston nodded, too, and eased away from her. While he waited for her explanation, he checked the Saturday-night special.

"Forget something?" he asked, showing her the empty chambers. The gun wasn't even loaded.

"I didn't want to hurt you. I only wanted answers."

This was getting more and more confusing with each passing moment. "And you thought this was the way to get them? Guess a phone call or e-mail would be too simple?"

"Too risky," she mumbled.

Okay, that got his interest. "Why?"

"Because I knew you'd just let them know where I was. Please, call them off. Tell them what you did was a mistake. Don't try to take him away from me. Please, don't." The tears started to stream down her cheeks again.

Well, he'd demanded an explanation and had gotten one…of sorts. But Houston still didn't have a clue who she meant by "them" or "him." Was she talking about her brother now? Was someone after Gabrielle and him?

Before he could press for clarification about the mistake she thought he'd made, he heard his ranch foreman, Dale Burnett, call out to him.

"Houston? You in there?"

He also heard Dale's footsteps coming straight for the stables. His ranch foreman wasn't alone, either. There were at least two sets of footsteps.

"The sheriff's with me," Dale added. "He says it's important and he needs to speak to you."

Gabrielle immediately ducked behind a tack shelf. "Please, don't tell anyone I'm here," she whispered. She added another "please," and he saw the color blanch from her face. Her fingers trembled as she caught onto the shelf.

Hell.

Again, Houston cursed his upbringing. He was a sucker for a pretty little thing in trouble, and while Gabrielle and he might have had their differences, she was indeed in trouble.

Even though he figured he'd regret this, Houston shoved her gun into the back waist of his jeans and walked to the stable entrance to meet Dale and Sheriff Jack Whitley.

Dale's weathered face was ripe with concern, and he looked at Houston as if he had answers. Houston didn't. But he hoped to remedy that soon.

"Mr. Sadler," the sheriff said, in greeting.

"Houston," he offered, for the umpteenth time, though he figured the sheriff would probably never call him by his first name.

None of the townsfolk in Willow Ridge did. That was almost certainly due to Houston's surly father and grandfather who made sure everybody knew the Sadlers were stinkin' rich and should therefore be respected.

"What can I do for you, sheriff?"

Sheriff Whitley didn't jump right into an explanation. In fact, he looked downright uncomfortable when he turned to Dale. "Could you give Mr. Sadler and me some time to talk, alone?"

Dale looked at Houston, and he gave his ranch foreman a nod, to let him know he could leave.

"Is someone hurt?" Houston demanded, the moment Dale walked away. "Dead?"

"No. But I just got a visit from two detectives from the San Antonio Police Department. It's related to the maternity hostage situation that happened at the hospital about six weeks ago. You remember it?"

"Of course." It'd been all over the news. Masked gunmen had stormed into the San Antonio Maternity Hospital and held a group of women hostage for hours. People died, including a cop's wife. If Houston remembered correctly, the gunmen had been killed in a shootout with the police, but there were rumors that they might have had an accomplice who was still at large.

"One of the former hostages, a woman, is missing, and SAPD wants to question her," the sheriff explained.

While that sounded like a serious problem, Houston wanted to hurry up this conversation so he could finish his little chat with Gabrielle.

"You don't think the gunmen's accomplice or the missing woman is around Willow Ridge or the ranch, do you?" Houston asked.

The lanky sheriff shook his head, paused again. "SAPD and the FBI don't have actual proof that there *was* an accomplice. They don't know where the woman is, either, but you might be able to help with that."

Houston glanced at Gabrielle to make sure she was staying put. She was. But he didn't think it was his imagination that she was even more alarmed than she had been before the sheriff's arrival.

"How do you think I can help?" Houston wanted to know.

The sheriff took a deep breath. "After the hostage situation ended, SAPD tested the DNA of the newborns left unattended in the nursery during any part of the standoff. When they got the results, they realized one baby boy didn't match *any* of the mothers, so they repeated the test. Those results came back yesterday. The first test wasn't wrong. The child didn't match any of the mothers. And now, one mother and one baby are missing."

Was the sheriff talking about Gabrielle? And was a baby snatcher peering out at him from the tack blankets?

"Is this woman involved with the gunmen and the hostage situation?" Houston asked.

"SAPD doesn't think so."

"I see," Houston mumbled. So, she might not have taken part in the hostage situation, but she wasn't completely innocent, either. "She took a kid who wasn't hers." There weren't enough gentlemanly bones in his body to stop him from turning Gabrielle in to the sheriff. He couldn't let her get away with kidnapping.

Houston looked at her, to let her know that, but she was frantically shaking her head.

"Well, the baby wasn't hers, not biologically, anyway,"

the sheriff explained, before Houston could speak. "But she did give birth to it."

Houston snapped his attention back to the sheriff. "Excuse me?"

"There was surveillance video of her going into the delivery room. And the baby's ID bracelet matched the one on the woman's wrist. The only reason the cops did a DNA test was that they wanted to be a hundred percent sure that the right mothers got the right babies. They hadn't expected anything like this to turn up."

Another glance at Gabrielle. She was no longer shaking her head. She was looking at him with the saddest doe eyes he'd ever seen.

That wouldn't work, either.

"This woman was a surrogate of some kind?" Houston asked, figuring he'd finally worked it out. Gabrielle had been a surrogate and had changed her mind about giving up the baby. However, that didn't explain why the cops and sheriff would think this had anything to do with him.

The sheriff nodded. "Her name is Gabrielle Markham, an attorney I think you had some dealings with."

"I know her," Houston admitted. "Did she break the law when she ran with the baby?"

"Maybe. The police are still investigating it, but she might have become a surrogate through illegal means. And she might have done that so she could have some leverage over *you*. If all that's true, then, yeah, it would be obstruction of justice to take the child."

Gabrielle made a soft gasp, and even though it was soft, Houston thought it might be laced with outrage.

The sheriff glanced past Houston and looked around

the stables. He even took a step forward, probably intending to go inside and have a closer look around to see what had made that sound. Soon, Houston would let him do just that. But he wanted to hear the rest of this little story first.

"How could Ms. Markham hope to gain any leverage over me with an illegal surrogacy?" Houston asked.

Sheriff Whitley met him eye-to-eye. "Mr. Sadler… Houston, this is going to be tough news for you to hear. I figured I should warn you about that upfront."

A lot of bad things went through Houston's mind, but he managed a nod. Oh, this wouldn't be good. In all his thirty-six years, the sheriff had finally called him by his first name, and his tone was that of pure sympathy.

The sheriff eased off his hat. "About five years ago, your late wife, Lizzy, and you used the Cryogen Clinic, in San Antonio, to harvest Lizzy's eggs so you'd have embryos for in vitro fertilization."

Houston held up his hand to stop the sheriff. "We did, but we never used the embryos. Well, not successfully anyway." They'd made a half dozen attempts, but in vitro had never worked for them.

Houston squeezed his hands into fists for several seconds, so he could hold on to his composure. Even now, more than three years later, it was hell talking about this.

"Your wife died of breast cancer," the sheriff finished for him.

"Yeah." And Houston left it at that. "So, what do our embryos have to do with Ms. Markham?"

The sheriff shook his head, mumbled something under his breath. "At this point, the police don't know if Ms. Markham stole the embryo or not. But you can understand why they want to take her into custody. And they darn sure want to learn what she's been up to, and where she's taken the baby."

The sheriff paused again. "Has she been in contact with you about any kind of payment?"

Houston tried to shrug, but he was getting a very bad feeling about this. "Why would she?"

"Maybe she wants to use the child to get you to cough up money?"

That bad feeling got significantly worse. Each word hit Houston like a fist. "Back up. Are you saying what I think you're saying?"

The sheriff took his time, and his forehead bunched up before he nodded. "I'm saying the baby boy that Gabrielle Markham gave birth to six weeks ago is your son."

Chapter Two

Gabrielle's instincts were to run, to get out of there as fast as she could. It'd been a terrible mistake, coming to Houston Sadler's ranch. Now, it might cost her the very thing she was trying desperately to hang on to, her baby, Lucas.

She looked at the back of the stables for a way out. There was a set of double doors, both closed, and Gabrielle only hoped they weren't locked—and that the big horse that Houston had ridden would get out of her way. While she was hoping, she added that neither the sheriff nor Houston would spot her while she escaped.

Gabrielle made her way behind the shelves and was about to climb over a stall when she heard the sound. It was a loud groan, so loud and so filled with emotion that it caused her to turn around. Houston had made that sound, and even though his back was to her, he had his head tilted toward the sky as if seeking divine help.

She understood his reaction.

Lately, Gabrielle had been doing her own share of praying.

"You're sure about this baby being mine?" Houston asked the sheriff.

"I'm sure. What SAPD hasn't figured out yet is how Ms. Markham got the embryo in the first place. Your wife hadn't left a signed agreement that it could be donated, so there's no legal way Ms. Markham could have used it. That's why SAPD is so concerned. They don't know what she intends to do with the baby."

That stopped Gabrielle in her tracks, and the anger slammed through her again. How dare they accuse her of doing anything wrong. She was the victim here, and Houston Sadler was the person who'd probably put this sick plan together.

At least she'd thought that when she sneaked onto the ranch and into the stables to wait for him.

When she'd come up with the idea to get Houston to confess to his dirty deeds, she'd been thankful that he was a man of routine. Just about everyone in Willow Ridge knew that Houston took his favorite horse out for a ride after lunch, so she'd delivered some flowers to the house and then made her way to the stables. The ranch was such a big operation, with dozens of employees, that no one had seemed to notice her, and no one had been in the stables to question why she was there.

Her plan had succeeded—except for the fact that she might have been wrong. Judging from that emotion-filled groan, Houston could be innocent. But Gabrielle wasn't ready to buy that just yet. He was the only one with a motive for making this pregnancy happen. Her only motive was that she'd desperately wanted a child and hadn't been able to have one of her own.

"Are you all right?" the sheriff asked him.

She couldn't hear what Houston mumbled, but if it was "yes," then it was a lie. Either he'd just learned for the first time that he was a father, or else he'd learned that his devious plan had been uncovered.

Gabrielle got moving again with her escape, because either scenario spelled trouble for her.

Houston glanced over his shoulder, and Gabrielle ducked down behind the stall door so he wouldn't see her. He didn't look around the stables for her. Instead, he turned his attention back to the sheriff.

"I need some time to think about this," Houston said, suddenly sounding more alert. "Don't say anything to my dad, just yet. But could you tell my foreman, Dale, what you told me, and let him know I'll be in the stables for a while?"

Gabrielle waited, with her pulse thick and throbbing. Was Houston really going to send the sheriff away? Or was this some kind of trick?

She cursed the fog in her head. If her thoughts were clearer, she might be able to figure out all of this, but she hadn't slept more than three hours straight in the past six weeks. Before that, there had been the delivery, immediately followed by the hostage situation. She was exhausted, spent and beyond punchy. Still, this might finally all come to a head. She might finally learn what was going on. If Houston would finally come clean.

Of course, that was a big *if*.

Houston waited until the sheriff walked away before he entered the stables. He shut the doors. And Gabrielle cursed again. Had she made yet another mistake by staying so she could get his side of the story? Or rather his side of the lie?

"Is it true?" Houston asked.

Gabrielle eased up so she could see him from over

the top of the stall—and was stunned by the raw feelings she saw there in his eyes. If Houston had indeed put all of this together, then he was a good actor.

She walked out of the hay-strewn stall so she could face him. But Gabrielle didn't get close. She didn't want him trying to kill her to cover up his plan. However, he didn't seem a man with murder on his mind.

That didn't mean he wasn't dangerous.

Even though he looked like an average cowboy, with his jeans, worn black leather vest and denim shirt with the sleeves rolled up, he also wore his privileged blood-line. It was there. In his glacier-blue eyes, and saddle-brown hair that was a little too long and messy for the boardroom, but perfect for a man who worked with both his hands and his mind.

Houston Sadler was a wealthy man. A billionaire. And he was accustomed to getting exactly what he wanted.

"Is it true?" he repeated.

Gabrielle hiked up her chin and forced herself to answer. "I did get pregnant through in vitro, but I didn't steal an embryo. I didn't steal anything."

"Except a baby from the nursery at the San Antonio Maternity Hospital," he quickly pointed out.

"*My* baby," she insisted.

In the same moment, Houston said, "I want to see him. I want to see *my* son."

Oh, God. This was exactly what she feared most. "Lucas is not your son. I gave birth to him."

He rammed his thumb against his chest. "With my late wife's embryo that you stole." He groaned again and shook his head. "I have a son."

She wasn't totally immune to that painful reaction.

Gabrielle almost went closer. Almost. But she forced herself to stop and think, even though her head felt foggier than it had when she'd started all of this.

"Because I'm infertile, I asked for a donor embryo from the Cryogen Clinic in San Antonio," Gabrielle explained. "I certainly never intended to have your child. But you, on the other hand, might have wanted exactly that. Did you set all of this up so I'd be your surrogate?"

He just stared at her for several long moments. "How the hell could you think that?"

"Well, it's one of the few theories that makes sense. Maybe, like me, you desperately wanted a baby, and you decided this was the way to go about it. You might have figured that, once I gave birth, you could step in and challenge me for custody. And then you'd have the child you always wanted with your wife."

Houston cursed, and it seemed to take him a moment to rein in his own fit of temper. "First of all, I'd forgotten about the embryos. I thought Lizzy and I had used them all on our last try at in vitro. And if I'd wanted a surrogate, I would have hired one—the best money could buy. I wouldn't have tricked you into it."

Gabrielle let that sink in. Slowly. And she repeated it to herself. It sounded…reasonable but it didn't explain everything.

"Someone's been following me since the hostage incident," she admitted. "I keep losing him, but then he pops up again. The last time, three days ago, the person used a dark green Range Rover."

Houston threw up his hands. "Maybe the gunmen from the hospital had an accomplice after all. Then again, it could be your imagination running wild. You seem to have a tendency to do that." He pointed his index finger at her. "Look, I don't care. Right now, I only want you to take me to my son."

"He's not yours!" she yelled. "Lucas is mine!"

The horse whinnied and pranced around, moving even farther toward the back of the stables.

Gabrielle immediately hated the outburst. She didn't want the sheriff and the foreman to hear her and come in after her. She didn't want to go to jail, because heaven knows how long it would take all of this to be settled. And in the meantime, the courts would no doubt give temporary and then permanent custody to Houston.

He had both biology and money on his side. Even though she hadn't stolen the embryo or manipulated the situation in any way, she might not be able to prove her innocence.

"Where is he?" Houston demanded.

"Someplace safe."

That was all she intended to tell him. She might not be able to keep Lucas from him forever, but she would try.

"Three days ago, I saw the license plates of the person who followed me," she explained. "The person driving that dark green Range Rover. And I took a picture of the plates with the camera on my cell phone. I had a friend run them through the database, and I learned the vehicle belongs to you."

"Me?" he challenged.

"You. And that's why I believe you're behind this. Why else would you follow me? The cops didn't have the latest DNA results until yesterday." That's when they'd called and left her a message on her work cell phone, even though they could have known earlier than that. "And they only *officially* told you about Lucas just now. So how did you know three days ago to follow me?"

He couldn't have, unless he'd known about all of this before today. "This doesn't make sense," Houston finally said.

For the first time since she'd heard those results, Gabrielle breathed a little easier. "No, it doesn't. And if I'm to believe that you had no part in this, then who else would have done it?"

His glare returned. "Maybe you. Maybe you figured I was your permanent meal ticket."

Now Gabrielle was the one to glare. They were right back where they started. It was clear she wasn't getting anywhere with this explanation or argument, and that meant it was time to leave.

Besides, she'd already been away from Lucas for nearly three hours, and it would take her thirty minutes or more to get back to him. She'd left breast milk in a bottle for the nanny to give him, but it wouldn't be long before her son wanted to nurse. Ditto for her. She could feel the pressure in her breasts, and that wrestling match with Houston hadn't helped matters.

"Lucas is my son," she said, under her breath. Only hers. And it would stay that way.

She turned and started to walk toward the back doors, but Houston latched on to her arm and spun her around.

"I *will* see him," he insisted.

Gabrielle decided to placate him—or rather, lie. "All

right. You can see him tomorrow morning. I'll call you with the address."

He didn't exactly roll his eyes, but it was close. However, the man's voice cut off another stinging remark he was obviously about to make.

"Houston?" the man called out, and the front stable doors flew open.

Gabrielle darted to the side, next to the stall, but instead of going in it where she'd be trapped, she ducked around the front and then behind the tack shelves again.

"Dad," Houston answered. "What do you want?"

Mack Sadler was an older, genetic copy of Houston. Houston didn't look at his father, but he angled his body so he could keep an eye on Gabrielle.

"I made the sheriff tell me what he told you," Mack announced. "Is it true? Did that Markham woman really steal one of those eggs Lizzy had stored and use it to give birth to your son?"

Houston blew out a long breath before he answered. "It seems that way."

Mack went closer, and Gabrielle used the sound of the man's footsteps to move farther behind the shelves. She began to inch her way toward the open doors. Maybe Houston's father would distract him long enough for her to get out of there. That was a long shot, of course, but it was the only one she had.

"Well, hell." Mack shook his head and propped his hands on his hips. "You gotta get the boy. He's a Sadler, and he belongs here at the ranch with us. Where is he?"

"I'm not sure," she heard Houston say.

"Then find him. Hell, *I'll* find him."

Gabrielle made it to the door, but Houston was staring at her.

"Don't worry, I intend to get the baby," he assured his father. "But for now, I need just a little time to come to grips with this." Houston paused, swallowed hard and tipped his head to the horse. "Could you see to Bear? I'm going for a walk."

His father didn't protest, though he did take his time looking at Houston before he started toward the horse. That was Gabrielle's cue to get moving again. She darted out from behind the tack shelves and bolted for the door.

She started running. And she didn't look back.

However, she didn't have to look back to hear the sound of the racing footsteps behind her. Houston was following her.

Gabrielle wasn't surprised. In fact, she'd expected it, but she had a good head start on him. She needed to make it to her car, which was still parked in front of the main house so she could try to drive away.

That wouldn't stop him.

Houston would continue to follow her; but if she could just get back onto the highway, she might be able to lose him. Then, she could pick up Lucas and the nanny and go into hiding again. This time, she wouldn't come out until she had all of this mess settled.

Gabrielle's heart pounded harder with each step. Her lungs felt ready to burst. She was out of shape and hadn't run since early in her pregnancy, but she used every bit of her energy and resolve to race across the yard and to the front. Thankfully, she'd left the car unlocked, and she jerked open the door and dove inside. Not so thankfully, her keys were in her pocket, and she had to dig for them.

She finally pulled them free, jammed the key into the ignition and started the car. She had barely touched the accelerator, when the passenger door flew open and Houston jumped inside.

"Keep going," Houston demanded.

He wasn't breathing hard and certainly didn't look as if he'd just sprinted across his massive yard. But he did look intense. Eyes narrowed. Mouth tight. His jaw muscles were working hard against each other.

"I said keep going," he repeated. "Drive. Take me to my son. Or I'll call the sheriff and have him arrest you right now."

Oh, God. Some choice. Revealing her son's location or jail.

If she went to jail, it was all over. The nanny, Lily Rose, would eventually start making calls to find out where she was. That would in turn lead the police to Lucas. Then Houston would take him.

But if she pretended to cooperate with Houston, it might buy her some time.

Gabrielle put on her seat belt and drove away from the ranch. Houston put on his belt, too, and then turned to face her.

"I figure you're up to something," he accused. "You're trying to decide the best way to ditch me. That's not going to happen, Gabrielle. I didn't come up with this so-called plan to produce a baby, but the child exists now, and I won't walk away from him."

Gabrielle knew she should just shut up, but she

couldn't make herself stop. "You might have to walk away when I prove you orchestrated this. I took a picture of the car that followed me, the one registered to you."

He stayed quiet a moment. "Then why not just go to the police?"

"I considered it. But then I decided you'd have some kind of explanation, or enough cops in your pocket, that I'd be the one who ended up in jail."

"I don't own any cops, and there are several logical explanations. Someone could have used fake license plates. Or maybe the photo isn't clear and you had your friend run the wrong numbers. Stating the obvious, again, but you could also be lying because you think I'll give you a big payout for giving birth to Lizzy's and my baby."

Gabrielle huffed and took the turn to the farm road that would lead her to the highway. From there, she would take the interstate south, the opposite direction she'd need to go if she had any intentions of driving Houston to see Lucas.

"I didn't lie," she insisted, though she knew it wouldn't do any good.

"How much money did you plan to ask for?" Houston wanted to know.

"None. Because Lucas is not for sale."

Houston obviously ignored that. "How much? Because you know what? As much as this disgusts me, I'll give you fifty million for him."

She made a sound of outrage.

"Seventy-five million," Houston countered.

That did it. Thankfully, there wasn't anyone behind her because Gabrielle slammed on her brakes. Her tires squealed in protest, and she brought the car to a jarring halt amid the fumes and smoke of the rubber burning on the asphalt.

Gabrielle grabbed him by his shirt, gathering up wads of fabric in her fists, to make sure they would have a face-to-face conversation and complete eye contact. "I didn't have Lucas so I could sell him to you, or anyone else. I had him because I've wanted a baby my entire life, and I didn't want to wait until Mr. Right showed up so I could have a traditional family. Lucas is my family now. Your late wife might be his biological mother, but I carried him for nine months. I gave birth to him."

She fought it, but the emotion clogged her throat, making her voice a whisper. Tears sprang to her eyes. "He's my baby, and I won't let you take him."

Houston opened his mouth, probably to return verbal fire, but he stopped and glanced behind them. When he didn't bring his gaze to hers, Gabrielle looked to see what had captured his attention.

It was a black car.

And it had come to a stop about thirty yards behind them.

"Is that the same car that you said was following you, the one that belongs to me?" he asked.

Gabrielle turned fully in the seat so she could get a better look. Not that she needed it.

She recognized the black car with the heavily tinted windows. That tint made it impossible to see the driver or anyone else who might be in the vehicle.

"No. I told you that was a Range Rover," she clarified. "The one behind us is a different vehicle, but I have seen it before."

"When and where?" he snapped.

She fought through the fog in her head so she could remember. "The first time was the day I took Lucas home from the hospital."

"The day you stole him."

That should have given her another jolt of anger, but she was too concerned about that menacing vehicle behind them. "I didn't steal him. After the hostage situation ended, the police had completed the DNA test on him, and I figured we were free to go. My mistake was in not telling the police that I used a donor embryo. Needless to say, I wasn't thinking straight after being held at gunpoint for hours."

"But you had something to hide," Houston reminded her. "Because you went on the run."

"Yes, because of that car back there. I thought it was following me, and I was afraid it might be someone involved with the hostage situation."

"An accomplice?" he questioned.

She nodded. "I figured that was a strong possibility, so I asked for police protection. They didn't have the resources to provide a round-the-clock guard, but they did say they would send an officer to patrol my neighborhood. I didn't think that was enough."

He made a sound that was possibly an agreement. If he'd lived through the hostage situation as she had, he wouldn't have thought it was enough, either.

"I lost sight of the car that day," she continued, "but it reappeared about a week later, outside the hotel where I was staying. That's when I changed locations." And why she continued to change.

The fear started to grow. That same fear that'd caused Gabrielle to be on the run for the past six weeks. "Please tell me you know who's in that car. Is it someone who works for you?" she asked, hoping.

"No." And Houston didn't hesitate, either. He took out his phone.

Gabrielle grabbed his wrist to stop him. "If you call the sheriff, he'll take me into custody for questioning. Maybe he'll even arrest me for what the cops think is an illegal surrogacy. If I'm arrested, you'll never find Lucas."

Houston volleyed glances between the car and her. The vehicle started to inch its way toward them. "You said you had Lucas hidden safely away?"

"Yes. Of course," she answered, cautiously.

"Good. Because that's not one of my vehicles back there, but it could belong to someone connected to the hostage situation."

Her fear went up another notch, even though she'd already been through this mentally a hundred times. "But why follow me? If they want to eliminate a potential witness, why not just try to kill me?"

"Maybe because they haven't had the right opportunity. Maybe they wanted to wait to kill you when they figured there would be no one around to see. Like now, for instance, when you're on a deserted country road."

Oh, God. He could be right.

"Start driving," Houston instructed. "But keep your speed down."

She glanced at the car, nodded and got her own vehicle moving. Thankfully, the black vehicle stayed put.

"If the gunmen did have an accomplice, would he have known that you had a child?" Houston asked her.

Gabrielle didn't have to think long about that.

"Probably. Lucas was born in the hospital not long after the gunmen stormed the place. After I delivered him, the gunmen made the nurse take him and put him in the nursery because they wanted all the babies in one place."

She shuddered and bit her bottom lip to keep those nightmarish memories at bay.

Houston cursed and shook his head. "Could this accomplice know that he's my son?"

She started to say no, but the truth was, Gabrielle had no idea, because she didn't know who these people following her were. She'd been a lawyer long enough to know that leaks happened. Information could be misdirected. And people could be bribed.

"Oh, God," she whispered.

"Yeah," Houston agreed. "There could be a good reason why the accomplice hasn't already killed you. They might want you to lead them to Lucas. That way, they have you, Lucas and about a billion dollars they can demand for my son's ransom."

Gabrielle's gaze flew to the rearview mirror.

The black car was coming right at them.

Chapter Three

Houston wanted to curse. How the hell had he let this situation come to this?

He should have tackled Gabrielle when she ran from the barn, or else forced her to stay put while he made arrangements to go and get the baby. He damn sure shouldn't be sitting on a backcountry road with would-be kidnappers who might be ready to pounce.

A billion dollars was lot of motive to get a potential kidnapper to force Gabrielle into revealing Lucas's location. God knows what they would do to her to get the information they wanted.

Houston laid his phone on the dash so his hands would be free. "Do you have ammunition for this?" he asked, taking the Saturday-night special from the back waist of his jeans.

She gave a shaky nod but didn't take her eyes off the black car behind them. "In the glove compartment."

Houston jerked it open and started to load the gun.

"What should I do?" she wanted to know.

"Keep driving." Not that he thought that would solve their problem. The car would probably continue to follow them. But anything was better than just sitting there waiting for the worst to happen.

Houston finished loading the gun then he grabbed his phone.

"No!" she insisted. "You can't call the sheriff. What if he's in on this? If the DNA information was indeed leaked to the men following us, he might have been the one to do it."

"I don't believe that."

"Well, as a minimum, he told your father about Lucas, something you asked him to keep to himself."

"True. But you don't know my father. He can be a very persuasive man. He probably convinced the sheriff I was on the verge of suicide or something."

Sheriff Whitley was decent and honest. But Houston didn't know his deputies nearly as well. Or any of the people who worked in the sheriff's office. One of them could be in on this, and Gabrielle was right—a call to the sheriff might be giving yet more information to the wrong people.

"I'll hold off calling him for now," Houston let her know. He angled the visor so he could use the attached vanity mirror to keep watch on the car behind them. As expected, it was still there. "But I need to talk to Dale, my foreman."

"You can trust him?"

"If I couldn't, he wouldn't be working for me," Houston said, assuring her. He scrolled through the names, hit the call button, and Dale answered on the first ring.

"You okay?" his foreman immediately asked.

"For now. But I got a problem and I need your help.

This stays between us, got that? Not a word of it to my father."

"I understand. What do you need me to do?"

"First, I want you to get two ranch hands, ones you trust. Ones who are good with a gun and can keep a calm head. Have them take one of the trucks and drive out to Farm Road six six one, so they can follow me. I'm in Gabrielle Markham's blue Ford. She's the one who just drove away from the ranch. We've got someone who's tailing us, and I'd like a chance to talk to that someone."

Dale's breathing was suddenly audible. So was Gabrielle's, and she gripped on to the steering wheel so hard that she'd likely have bruises. She was scared and had good reason to be.

Hell, he was scared, too.

Not for himself. Not even for her. But for the son he'd just learned he had.

Later, he would have to come to terms with that. Later, he'd celebrate and file away all the emotions and old pain that was now right at the surface. Lizzy and he finally had the baby they'd always wanted, and that baby was at risk.

"Houston, are you okay?" Dale repeated.

"I will be when you get those ranch hands out here. Don't call Sheriff Whitley yet. Instead, phone my old friend, Jordan Taylor, the security specialist in San Antonio, and have him run the license plate, VSM seven six eight," he read from the black car that was following them. "And I need you to do one final thing."

"Just say the word."

In some ways, this would be the most unsavory request

of all. But it was a necessary one. "Check through the records of the ranch's vehicles and see who last used the green Range Rover and when."

"Will do," Dale assured him. "I'll call you when I have news, and I'll get help out to you right away."

Houston hung up and put the phone on the seat next to him so he could reach it in a hurry.

"Which way should I go?" Gabrielle asked, drawing Houston's attention back to her. The sign ahead pointed to the turn for the highway.

"Stay on this road," Houston instructed.

It was deserted, which meant there would be no one around to help if those guys started shooting, but he knew this road like the back of his hand, and Gabrielle and he might need to take one of the old ranch trails if necessary. That would be a last option, but Houston wanted to keep that possibility available.

"If that's the gunmen's accomplice back there and he's really after Lucas, then he won't kill us," he tried to assure Gabrielle.

Not intentionally, anyway. But such an accomplice would likely want to keep Gabrielle alive only so they could get Lucas's location.

Which she probably wouldn't give up.

So they could indeed kill her, and then figure out another way to get the child. Houston was expendable, too, because they could always get the money from his father, who was wealthy in his own right. But Houston didn't want to let things get that far.

Best to stop this now, so he could go about seeing his son.

Gabrielle sucked in her breath. "They're speeding up."

Because Houston had his attention nailed to the other vehicle, he noticed it immediately.

Gabrielle sped up, too.

That was all right for now; but within two miles or so, there were some deep curves, and Houston didn't want her losing control of the car and slamming into the thick trees that lined the road.

Houston got the gun ready, just in case. He watched the black car come closer. And closer. It was closing in on them fast.

"Brace yourself," Houston warned Gabrielle.

But the words had hardly left his mouth when the black car bashed into their rear bumper. The jolt tossed them forward, a fierce jerking motion that caused his teeth to hit together. He tried to steady himself and kept a tight grip on the gun.

"You'll have to slow down ahead," Houston warned her.

The car rammed into them again.

Houston heard the scream bubble up in Gabrielle's throat, but she clamped on to her lip to stop the full sound. She was obviously terrified. So was he. If they both died right here, right now, what would happen to his son?

Gabrielle did as he asked and slowed down, which only made the next jolt even harder. The black car was bigger, and obviously, the driver wasn't concerned about damage, because he bashed into them again. And again.

This time though, the car didn't fall back to launch

another assault. It stayed pressed right against their bumper, and the driver sped up.

The SOB was trying to make them crash. And with those curves ahead, he just might succeed.

"Hit your brakes." Houston had to yell over the sound of the metal grinding against metal.

Gabrielle did, and that kicked up a curtain of smoke and sparks. But they still didn't stop. The black car kept propelling them forward, even though it was now a slow, creeping speed.

Houston quickly thought of the road that lay ahead, and just on the other side of the upcoming curve, there was a ranch trail to the right. It was wide enough for Gabrielle to turn onto safely.

He hoped.

Then, maybe she could get far enough ahead on the trail so that they could stop and try to protect themselves. If he could get some cover, like an outcropping of rocks or a cluster of trees, he'd be able to make a stand. Against who or what exactly, he didn't know, and that bothered him. Houston had no idea if he was up against one or many, because it was hard to see through the tint on the windshield. It was also possible that some of the car's occupants could have ducked down and out of view.

The smoke from the brakes and tires was so thick now that he could hardly see the car behind them, but he could feel it. The driver was trying to push them to the right, off the road. And for now, Houston would use that to his advantage.

"Turn onto that trail about fifty yards away," he told Gabrielle. "It's on the right."

She shook her head. "I don't see it."

"You will," he promised.

Houston wanted to remind her that his ranch hands were on the way, that they'd soon have backup. But backup might not arrive in time to do any good. Thankfully, there'd be enough tire treadmarks on the road that his men wouldn't have any trouble finding them.

"There," Houston told her, when he spotted the trail.

Since Gabrielle's foot was already jammed onto the brake pedal, all she had to do was turn the steering wheel. The driver of the other car must have realized what was happening, because he made one last attempt to slam into them. Gabrielle took her foot off the brakes, and the momentum shot them forward on the dirt-and-gravel path.

"Hit the gas," Houston instructed.

She did, and what was left of the tires kicked up rocks and gravel and spewed the debris back toward the black car. Houston saw their windshield crack, the broken safety glass webbing across the entire surface. However, what he still couldn't see was the driver or any gunmen who might also be in the vehicle.

Gabrielle kept going, tearing her way through the trail that was little more than a path. Tree branches slapped against the car, and rocks battered like gunfire against the undercarriage.

"They stopped," Houston mumbled. But he held his breath, waiting. Because maybe it was just temporary.

"Are they coming?" Gabrielle asked. She had her attention nailed to the trail ahead. Good thing, too, because she had to jerk the steering wheel hard to the left when a deer darted right in front of them.

Houston stared at the black car. "No. Stop up ahead by those rocks."

"You want me to *stop?* Are you crazy? We're getting away from them."

"Yeah. And if we do that, it just means they'll try this again. And again. It's been my experience that people get pretty tenacious when there's a lot of money involved."

"Right," she finally answered, and pumped her brakes to bring the car to a stop.

Once the dust settled, Houston had no trouble seeing the black car. It sat there like a jungle cat ready to attack. But Houston was ready, too. He opened the glove compartment so he could get to the extra ammunition, and aimed the gun at the vehicle.

No one got out. They just sat there. And the moments crawled by.

When Houston's lungs began to ache, he realized he was holding his breath, so he forced himself to relax. He was a good shot—had even won some shooting competitions in his teens—and if necessary, he would kill these attackers if they came after Gabrielle and him.

But they didn't come.

The black car's engine roared to life, and the driver threw the vehicle into Reverse. He headed off the trail fast, and back toward the road.

"What should we do?" Gabrielle asked. Her voice was strained and practically soundless.

Houston considered going after them, but he had a better idea. He grabbed his phone and called Dale.

"How far out are the ranch hands?" Houston asked his foreman.

"They left a good five minutes ago."

Then they'd be here soon. "Tell them to follow the black car I told you about. And they'd better not lose sight of it. I want to know where that driver goes. If the car stops anywhere, I want to know about it." He didn't want these SOBs going anywhere near Lucas.

Wherever that was.

"Hang on the line, and I'll tell them," Dale assured him.

Houston heard Dale make the call and give the ranch hands the instructions to follow. Good. The driver of that black car wouldn't know that these men worked for Houston, and maybe, just maybe, he would soon have answers.

"You're sure you have Lucas someplace safe?" Houston asked Gabrielle.

She nodded. "No one except the nanny and I know where he is."

Gabrielle sounded confident enough, but Houston wasn't willing to take that chance. If the car went near where Lucas could be, he'd have the ranch hands stop them, one way or another.

"I called your friend, Jordan Taylor," Dale said, when he came back on the line with Houston. "The plates on that black car are bogus."

That wasn't a surprise. It was clear the driver had criminal intent on his mind, and he wouldn't want to advertise his real identity.

"And I checked the computer records on the ranch's vehicles. It only took a couple of seconds, because they're all linked to a central GPS."

That had been Dale's idea, so he would know when

all the vehicles were scheduled for maintenance, and which were available for use at any given moment.

"And?" Houston said, when Dale didn't continue.

Beside him, Gabrielle's breath was gusting. She was mumbling what sounded like a prayer. But Houston kept his attention nailed to their surroundings, in case the black car returned.

"The green Range Rover's only been taken out once in the past month, and that was three days ago," Dale finally continued. But the man hesitated again.

Hell. Someone had used it. And whoever it was had used it to follow Gabrielle, just as she'd said. What Houston wanted to know now was why the person had done that.

"And?" Houston snarled. "Who took the Range Rover off the ranch?"

Dale cleared his throat. "Your father."

Chapter Four

"This really isn't a good idea," Gabrielle reminded Houston, *again*.

Like the other reminders that she'd doled out in the past ten minutes since Houston had gotten behind the wheel of her car, this one didn't do any good, either, because he continued to drive toward his ranch. It was the last place in Texas she wanted to be, after hearing the news from Dale that Mack Sadler had driven the ranch's Range Rover on the very day that someone had used it to follow her. She didn't want to see or confront Mack just yet.

Besides, she needed to get back to Lucas.

She'd assured Houston that Lucas was safe from the people in that black car, but Gabrielle didn't want to risk being away from him any longer. She also didn't want to press the point of getting back to the baby, because that would only spur Houston into demanding that he go along with her. So she tried a different angle.

"Someone just tried to run us off the road," Gabrielle said. "Maybe this time he didn't use the green Range Rover. Maybe Mack used another vehicle from the ranch."

"My father had nothing to do with what just happened," Houston snapped. He had his attention fastened to the road ahead, and every muscle in his face was iron hard.

"Right," she mumbled. "Then who was it?"

His jaw muscles tightened even more, something she hadn't thought possible. "I don't know, but I sure as hell intend to find out."

She didn't doubt that he would try to do that. Houston was invested in this now. Unfortunately.

He knew about Lucas, and he wasn't just going to forget that he had a biological son. That meant Gabrielle would have to go on the run again. Somehow, she'd have to hide.

A pang of guilt hit her harder than she'd expected.

Lucas was indeed Houston's son, and that perhaps did give him some legal rights, but she couldn't let him be part of her baby's life. The incident with the black car was a stark warning that Lucas's safety had to come first.

The problem was, how could she outrun the danger?

Gabrielle had some savings, but it wasn't unlimited, and it would be eaten up quickly if she had to use it for hotels and travel. She didn't have any rich relatives, either. Her brother, Jay, lived from paycheck to paycheck, when and if he was working, and he wasn't what anyone would consider responsible.

She was on her own, and obviously in deep trouble.

"My father wasn't in that black car," Houston mumbled. "He also wouldn't have done anything to make you an unwilling surrogate. And he would have no reason to follow you three days ago. Whoever took that photo of the license plates made a mistake."

Was it her imagination, or did he seem to be trying to convince himself?

Still, it didn't make sense that Mack would risk hurting his own son in a car crash. For that matter, Mack's possible involvement with her didn't make sense, either. She'd never met the man, and he'd had nothing to do with the lawsuit involving her brother.

So, did that mean someone had set up Mack to make him look guilty?

It was a good theory, except that Gabrielle couldn't think of a reason for that, either. If this had something to do with a possible accomplice of the gunmen who'd taken her hostage, then how did that connect back to the Sadlers?

Maybe it didn't.

But Gabrielle wasn't about to declare either of them innocent just yet. The only thing she knew was that her routine request for a donor embryo had somehow turned into a nightmare—a nightmare that had produced a baby she loved more than life itself.

Houston turned into the driveway that led to the front of the ranch house. Except, it was really more of a sprawling mansion than a mere house. It was three stories, all pristine white, with porches and columns that stretched across the front on all three levels. It was yet another reminder that, if it came down to a custody battle, it wouldn't be easy to fight Houston and his money.

Dale was waiting for them on the first-floor porch, and he hurried out to the car the moment Houston brought it to a stop. "Are you okay?" he asked Houston, and then looked at Gabrielle, as well.

She nodded, but Houston didn't respond, and instead asked, "Where's Dad?"

"Inside his office, waiting. I told him you'd asked about the Range Rover."

Houston shoved her gun into the glove compartment and slammed the car door, perhaps not pleased that Dale had even brought up the subject with the senior Sadler. Or maybe that was just Gabrielle's take on things. Houston's reaction could have stemmed from the fact that he was still fuming from the attack.

No fuming for her, but she was still shaking. Gabrielle hoped she could hold herself together long enough to get the heck out of there.

First though, she was apparently about to see Mack.

Then, when she was away from the ranch and the Sadlers, she could fall apart and have a good cry.

"I didn't call the sheriff, just as you asked, and I sent the two ranch hands after the black car," Dale explained, as they stepped onto the porch.

"Did they find it?" Houston asked.

"They did, and they're keeping a close watch on it."

Gabrielle groaned softly. She didn't want them to keep a close watch. She wanted the driver of that vehicle apprehended, so she could finally learn why she'd been followed and harassed in the six weeks since Lucas's birth. Of course, if the sheriff arrested the men in that car, she would have to come out of hiding to give her statement about what they had done.

Talk about being between a rock and a hard place. Either decision could be a dangerous one.

Houston opened the double front doors and ushered her inside. The entrance was just as grand as the rest of the house, as was each room they passed along the way to his father's office. Houston stopped outside a closed door, and he glanced at her, then Dale.

"Why don't you take Gabrielle to the kitchen and fix her a cup of tea or something?" Houston asked his foreman.

Gabrielle was shaking her head before Houston even finished. "I don't want any tea. I want to hear what your father has to say for himself." She made certain that her tone left no room for argument. The sooner they had this conversation, then the sooner she could leave.

Houston stared at her for several moments. "Call the ranch hands and find out the latest on the car they're following," he instructed Dale. "I don't want the driver of that vehicle to make any stops anywhere near the baby. Understand?"

Dale assured him that he would, and the man walked away, leaving Houston and her still staring at each other. She braced herself for him to open the door and confront his father, but he didn't.

"Are you okay?" he asked.

Gabrielle blinked. His expression was so different than it had been on the drive over. No more iron muscles in his face, and his eyes no longer seemed so icy.

"I wasn't hurt," she clarified.

"Not even when I wrestled the gun away from you in the stables?"

She thought of that contact between. Yes, he'd been rough, but it could have been a lot worse. Maybe it was her imagination, but Houston seemed to have treated her with kid gloves. Gabrielle wasn't sure she would have been that gentle with him if their positions had been reversed.

"When I came after you like that," he continued, "I didn't know you'd recently given birth."

He was worried about hurting her, which was considerate. After all, she'd pulled a gun on him—something she would regret for the rest of her life. But she wouldn't regret the anger if she learned Houston was behind all of this. If he had done this to her on purpose, then she would somehow make him pay.

"You didn't hurt me," she settled for saying.

"Good." A moment later, Houston asked, "Are you still recovering from the delivery?"

"No. I didn't have a C-section, so I was back on my feet almost right away."

And that seemed like way too much information to be sharing with him. Houston Sadler didn't have the right to know anything about her personal welfare, other than that she was capable of taking care of Lucas on her own.

"But you must have had some health problems," he said, "or you wouldn't have had to use a donor embryo."

"I'm sterile because of chemo I had to have when I was a kid." *Again, way too much information.* "And I'd rather not talk about that."

The silence turned awkward in a hurry, and Gabrielle didn't like that he suddenly seemed to be feeling sorry for her, or for what he'd done. This was essentially war between them, and she wanted to hang on to every drop of the anger, because it would fuel her for the inevitable battle with the Sadlers.

Houston looked as if he might add something else, but then he shook his head, knocked once and opened the door.

Mack was standing behind his grand oak desk with the bay windows framing him from behind. He had several shots of liquor in a cut crystal glass and took at least one of those shots in one gulp.

"Dale said somebody tried to run you off the road," Mack greeted. His attention landed on Gabrielle. "Was it because of her?"

"We're not sure," Houston answered.

"Well, son, we'd better find out because now that you know she's got your boy, you can't let anything happen to him."

Gabrielle had to bite her tongue. She hated that this arrogant man felt he had the right to dictate anything about Lucas. Lucas was hers!

"How you handling things?" Mack asked Houston.

By "things," he no doubt meant Lucas. But Houston didn't even address that.

He put his hands on his hips and stared at his father. "Dale told you about the green Range Rover."

"He did. What's that all about? Why does it matter if I drove it or not?"

Gabrielle didn't wait for Houston. She jumped right in with her answer. "Three days ago, someone driving a Range Rover followed me. A PI friend traced the plates to one of your ranch vehicles."

"I see." Mack had another gulp of the liquor. "And you think it was me?"

"Was it?" she demanded.

Mack didn't jump to deny it. "I used the Range Rover," he calmly admitted. "It was the anniversary of my wife's death, and I just wanted to get out for a while. I drove into San Antonio, to the Menger Bar, and had a few drinks. Last I heard, that wasn't a crime."

He was denying his guilt, and that shot her anger through the roof. "You followed me. Why?"

Gabrielle expected Houston to jump in and tell her to back off, that his father was innocent, but he didn't. He, too, stared at his father and waited for an answer.

Mack took a deep breath and eased into the chair behind his desk. However, he didn't address Gabrielle's question. Instead, he looked at Houston. "I was worried about you, son. It's been three years since Lizzy died, and you haven't moved on with your life."

Everything inside Gabrielle went still.

Houston apparently had the opposite reaction. "What the hell does that mean?" he snarled.

Mack dodged his son's glare and slowly ran his finger around the rim of his glass. "It means I wanted to help you." He paused. "And I did."

She felt the knot form in her stomach, and Gabrielle slid her hand over it. It didn't soothe her. Nothing would at this point. Her entire body was bracing itself for what Mack was about to say.

"How did you help?" Houston demanded.

Mack finished his drink, taking the rest in one gulp. "Almost a year ago, when you were out, you got a call from the Cryogen Clinic, the place where Lizzy had stored those embryos y'all were using before she got the cancer. I was worried the call would upset you, so I pretended to be you so they'd tell me what the problem was. They said there'd been a serious mixup."

Houston shook his head. "What kind of mixup?"

Gabrielle could only stand there and listen. The knot tightened, and her breath began to race.

"Lizzy hadn't signed an agreement," Mack continued, "but the only embryo of hers that was left was accidently donated to someone. So I drove over there to talk to Salvador Franks, the head of the clinic. He didn't want to tell me who'd gotten the embryo, but I said if he didn't I'd sue him into bankruptcy. That's when I learned Gabrielle here was the one who got it."

Houston groaned and pushed his hands against the sides of his head. "You knew? All this time you knew?"

He took the words right out of her mouth. But she already knew the answer. Mack had indeed known, practically since the moment she'd become pregnant.

But the question was, what had he done about it?

"Why the hell didn't you tell Gabrielle or me?" Houston demanded.

"I couldn't tell you because you would have gone to her and spilled everything." Mack got to his feet. "I knew she hated you. I thought she might do something to end the pregnancy."

"Never," Gabrielle snapped.

And she wouldn't have. But she would have liked the time to come to terms with what had happened. She'd planned the entire pregnancy around a donor embryo and figured she would never know the identity of the couple who had given her such a precious gift. And that was exactly the way Gabrielle had wanted it.

Mack aimed his index finger at her. "You say that now, but you would have been riled to the core to learn about the screwup at Cryogen."

Riled, yes. But not riled enough to end the pregnancy. She'd planned this pregnancy for years.

"Salvador Franks and I worked out a deal," Mack added. "He agreed not to tell anyone about Gabrielle getting the wrong embryo. Now SAPD is investigating the whole damn thing, and Franks is trying to cover his butt. I figure he's putting the blame on Gabrielle."

She looked at Houston, and his gaze slowly came to hers. There. She saw it: the shock and the hurt. He wasn't faking that, and that meant he probably hadn't known about any of this before now.

That didn't help.

It only meant Houston was another wounded party in all of this, but it didn't change the fact that she had indeed given birth to his and his late wife's son.

"You planned to buy off Gabrielle," Houston stated, turning a glare to his father. "You thought you could buy the baby from her."

"Well, after she defended her worthless brother the way she did, I didn't think she was a woman of principle," Mack answered. "I figured I could offer her enough money to hand over the baby to us."

Houston was as obviously stunned as she was, because they both just stood there and listened.

"That's why I've been following her," Mack continued. "Or trying to, anyway. That woman's like a cat with nine lives. She kept getting away from me. But I learned that SAPD had done DNA tests on the babies after that hostage mess, and I figured it was a matter of time before the cops figured out the boy was yours. Then, I knew I could bargain with Gabrielle."

So it hadn't been her imagination, as Houston had suggested. Someone *had* followed her since she'd left the hospital. That twisted the knot in Gabrielle's stomach even more.

"There's not enough money in the world to make me give up my baby to you or anyone else," Gabrielle told him.

She blinked back the tears, turned and hurried toward the door. She had to get out of there and back to Lucas.

"The boy belongs to Houston," Mack shouted out to her. "He's a Sadler and should be here with us."

Mack added something else, but Gabrielle couldn't make out his words. However, she could hear the footsteps behind her. It was no doubt Houston. But she didn't care to speak to him, either.

She started to sprint toward the front door. Her car was seriously damaged, but somehow it'd have to get her away from the ranch and back to San Antonio.

Gabrielle made it all the way to the foyer before Houston latched on to her arm and whirled her around to face him. The tears were blurring her vision but not enough that she couldn't see his stunned expression. It was identical to the one he'd had earlier when he learned that Lucas was his biological child.

Neither of them were having anything close to a good day, and under normal circumstances, Gabrielle might have actually felt sorry for him. But she had more to lose here. She'd carried Lucas, given birth to him and had taken care of him for the past six weeks. As cold and hard as it sounded, Houston didn't even know the baby.

She wanted to keep it that way.

"I had no idea my father knew about this," he said, the emotion straining his voice.

"I don't care." She tried to throw off his hand, but Houston held on. "None of this matters. Lucas is my son, not yours."

"But he *is* mine," Houston reminded her. "And even though I didn't have anything to do with what happened to you, I can't just let you walk out."

Gabrielle tried again to break free from him, but it was hard to do with the tears streaming down her cheeks. The raw sensations didn't help, either. She felt totally drained and defeated. But that couldn't last. She had to dig deep and fight her way out of this situation.

"I have to go," she insisted.

Gabrielle threw her weight back, so she could wrench herself out of his grip. And she succeeded. For a few seconds, anyway. Then Houston grabbed her by the shoulders and put her against the wall.

"I can't just let you walk out," he repeated.

A dozen different emotions went through her, and she pounded her fists against his chest. But Houston held on, pinning her in place with his body. He took every one of her punches. He just stood there and waited her out.

It didn't take long before Gabrielle spent what little energy she had left. The tears came harder now, and her hands dropped to her sides.

"I can't lose Lucas," she managed to say. "I love him. He's my life."

She waited for Houston to counter that with his own

argument, but he didn't. He stood there staring at her, and then he did something that shocked her.

He reached out and pulled her into his arms.

Gabrielle put up a token resistance. She pushed her shoulder against his, but she was too exhausted to fight him anymore. Her legs gave way, and if it hadn't been for Houston holding her, she would have slid straight to the glassy marble floor. She didn't want to take this comfort from him, but she did.

"You look like you're ready to pass out," he told her, his voice barely a whisper.

She was. Everything in the room started to spin. Gabrielle leaned into him and let him support her. For just a moment, she assured herself. This didn't mean anything, even though it was hard to forget that Houston Sadler was a man.

An attractive man at that. A man who was essentially her enemy. She forced herself to remember that. She couldn't rely on Houston for anything.

"My life is falling apart," she mumbled. "And someone tried to hurt us. Or worse." She stopped and considered that a moment. "Your father—"

"He didn't try to kill us today," Houston said. "That's what he was trying to tell you when you ran out of his office. He didn't hire the men who were in that black car."

Gabrielle shook her head. "He could be lying."

"Why would he lie about that? He told us the truth about what happened at the Cryogen Clinic."

"Only because I had proof that he'd followed me in the Range Rover. And because he must have guessed you would get to the bottom of this by going to Cryogen. You would have eventually learned what happened. Besides, if your father's plan was to try to buy the baby from me, then he would have had to come clean with you, once he had Lucas."

In fact, that's probably what Mack had been trying to do when he was following her. But Gabrielle had thwarted his plan because she'd managed to lose him and then move to a different hotel.

Losing him had been blind luck, though.

A minor car accident behind her vehicle and in front of the Ranger Rover had given her just enough time to turn onto a side street and then speed out of the area.

Houston met her eye-to-eye. "Look, right now I'm not sure I can ever forgive my father for what he did, but I don't think he wants me hurt or dead."

"No, he only wants a Sadler heir," she fired back.

He hissed out his breath. "If I had known about the embryo mixup, I would have told you."

"Would you have?" She didn't intend to give him any sympathy, though she wasn't totally untouched by the grief she saw on his face.

"I would have," he insisted. "I would have gone to you and worked something out."

That stayed between them for several moments. So did the eye contact. And Gabrielle cursed herself. Houston was pulling her in, and that couldn't happen.

He stepped back, away from her, and she immediately felt the loss. And his physical support. She had to brace her back against the wall to stop herself from falling.

Houston scrubbed his hand over his face and continued to stare at her. "Look, I'm as messed up as you are right now, but we have to think this through. Maybe the people who came after us today in that black car have to do with the person my father made the deal with at Cryogen. Maybe this guy is trying to put a lid on all of this."

Great. Another possible suspect.

Gabrielle started to shake her head but stopped. She'd assumed this had to do with the hostage situation. Or maybe it was someone who wanted to kidnap Lucas for ransom. But Houston was right. This could be related to the Cryogen Clinic. After all, the clinic head had committed a crime when he doctored her records and conspired with Mack to keep the truth about the illegally used embryo from Houston.

"I need to check and see where this threat is coming from," Houston said.

She considered telling him that she could do it herself, but she couldn't. Gabrielle didn't have the resources, and she couldn't very well go out in public and conduct her own investigation. Still, it was a risk to have Houston run this particular show. Mack was his father, and God knows what Houston would do to protect him.

"If you discover that your father is indeed behind this attempt to run us off the road—"

"Then I'll have him arrested. That applies to anyone else who tries to come after us again."

His words were suddenly so calm that Gabrielle studied him to make sure he was telling the truth. She wanted to believe he was. She wanted to believe that the danger and harassment might finally come to an end. But while his words were calm, Houston's expression wasn't.

His eyes were a dark, stormy blue.

"I swear, I'll get to the bottom of this," he promised. "But first you have to do something."

Gabrielle shook her head because she knew where this was leading.

He caught on to her face to stop the movement. "I'm not giving you a choice here, Gabrielle. You will take me to my son *now*."

Chapter Five

Houston forced himself to concentrate on the drive to the motel where Gabrielle had said Lucas and the nanny were staying.

Of course, she could be lying.

But a lie wouldn't stop him. If necessary, he'd bring SAPD and an entire team of private investigators into this. One way or another, he would see his son.

"Take this exit," Gabrielle instructed.

Her voice was practically hoarse, probably because she'd been fighting tears since they left the ranch. She had also said as little as possible. She was no doubt trying to decide the best way to get out of this.

Houston wanted to tell her there was no way out. Now that he knew the truth, he wasn't going to disappear into the woodwork. He would find his baby and get custody of him.

Hopefully.

He couldn't dismiss the fact that Gabrielle had been wronged in all of this. God knows how a court of law would interpret his father's involvement, but Houston would fight as long as it took to get his son.

"My son," he mumbled.

It didn't seem possible. All those months, Lizzy and he had tried to have a child, but after she'd gotten sick, they had given up. Truth was, he had given up on a lot of things after her diagnosis of terminal cancer. His father was right about that. He hadn't moved on with his life, but he would now. This baby was a miracle that he needed to put him in the right direction.

Lizzy's and his miracle.

Houston took a deep breath absorbing that, and then he glanced at Gabrielle out of the corner of his eye. She was slumped in the passenger's seat, leaning her head against the window, and she was staring at the side mirror.

She was obviously keeping watch, to make sure no one was following them. She was also upset, probably suffering from an adrenaline crash, too. While Houston was sympathetic to that, and to what his father had done, he couldn't let sympathy play a part in this.

Nor would he let Gabrielle take control of the situation and convince him to do things he wasn't ready and willing to do.

Despite her suspicions that his father might be responsible for the attempt to run them off the road, Houston didn't believe that for a minute.

No, there was something else going on here, and that was the reason he'd slipped a handgun into his jacket pocket. If those SOBs came at them again, Houston wanted to be prepared. That meant staying as close to Gabrielle as possible.

And staying close wasn't exactly comfortable for him.

He glanced at her again. At the way she'd tangled her

fingers into her hair. At the way her breathing strained her breasts against her top. At the way the sunlight danced off her pale skin.

Houston cursed himself and took his phone from his jacket pocket so he could call Dale. He needed to be thinking about more important things than hair and sunlight. Thankfully, Dale answered on the first ring.

"Any update from the ranch hands following that black car?" Houston asked.

"Not yet. The driver's just meandering around, and our men are following."

Houston hoped his men hadn't been spotted. "Meandering where, exactly?"

"South side of San Antonio."

That caused him to breathe a little easier. Gabrielle and he were on the opposite side of town. Of course, that didn't mean the baby wasn't on the south side, as well.

"Remember, if the car stops, I want to know about it," Houston reminded Dale, and they hung up.

"They still haven't caught the men in that black car?" she asked.

"No. And I don't want them caught just yet. I want to see where they're going. If it's anywhere near Lucas, my men will stop them." Houston waited but got no response. "Or maybe you think I should call the police and turn this whole matter over to them?"

She wearily shook her head. It was the reaction he'd expected. Gabrielle didn't want anything to do with SAPD, because, according to the sheriff, they thought she might be a suspect in the illegal surrogacy. She wasn't. But it would take time to clear that up, especially if the clinic head, Salvador Franks, had altered her records so that Gabrielle would get the blame for his clinic's screwup.

"Take the next left," Gabrielle told him.

Houston turned onto the street in a northeast neighborhood that was littered with budget hotels and fast-food restaurants. He caught the red light, the first of many that was at every intersection.

"The motel is one block up on the right. The Starlight Inn. But you should drive around for a couple of minutes," she insisted. "Just in case."

"That was my plan." Though he had been keeping watch, and Houston didn't think anyone was following them—including anyone his father might have sent—he wanted to be sure. That was one of the reasons they hadn't used Gabrielle's car, but rather one from the ranch.

The light changed to green, and Houston drove past the hotel. It wasn't easy to keep going. His son was inside—so close. But he forced himself to take the necessary precautions to keep the baby safe.

"What happens now?" Gabrielle asked.

Houston knew she wasn't talking about the drive. "I go in and meet my son."

She drew in a long breath. "Then what?"

He considered several possible answers but settled for "Then we talk."

Gabrielle blinked and eased her head in his direction. *"Talk?"*

Houston nodded and left it at that. Best not to bring up the whole subject of custody. He only wanted to focus on Lucas right now.

When Houston was certain they weren't being followed, he pulled into the parking lot of the Starlight Inn and stopped.

"Lucas is really here?" he asked Gabrielle.

"He's really here," she confirmed.

Houston looked at her. The emotion was still there, etched on her face. But something else was there, too.

That damn attraction simmering just below the surface.

He just couldn't get his mind off those brown eyes. Or that full mouth. Sheez. No woman should be allowed to have a mouth like that. It was a mouth that reminded him of kissing and other things he shouldn't want to do with her.

What the devil was wrong with him?

He couldn't let attraction or anything else play into this. The stakes were way too high for him to be thinking with any part of his body other than his brain.

"What?" she questioned. "Why are you looking at me like that?"

But Houston didn't even attempt to answer her question. He opened the car door and got out. "Which room?"

Gabrielle got out, as well, and walked to a room on the ground floor. All the rooms had exterior entrances, which meant they didn't have to go through a lobby.

She stopped in front of room 112 and lifted her hand as if she were about to knock, but then she stopped and stared at him.

"This is just a visit, understand," Gabrielle said. It wasn't a question. "You'll see him for a few minutes, and then you'll leave."

Not a chance. But Houston kept that to himself.

However, there was something he needed to clarify. "Why did you bring me here? Why didn't you just try to run again?"

She glanced away, paused. "I wanted to run and get as far away from you as possible," she admitted, "but after what happened with that black car today, I don't think I can outrun the danger, the cops, your father and you all at the same time. Right now, you're the lesser of the four evils, because at least I don't believe you're trying to hurt me or arrest me. Not yet, anyway," she added, in a mumble.

"I have no intention of hurting you," he promised. But kissing her and trying to protect her, well, that was a different story.

"Maybe not physically, but you and I both know you're in a position to destroy me. I can delay that. I can fight it. But I can't stop you from trying."

She didn't wait for him to respond to that heart-wrenching admission. Gabrielle gave three short knocks on the door. "It's me," she said, still looking over her shoulder.

Houston glanced over his, as well, and he heard someone undoing the locks. His heart rate and breathing instantly sped up, but he tried to rein in his emotions in case this was some kind of trick. He still wasn't convinced that Gabrielle had led him to the right place.

The petite Hispanic woman who opened the door was middle-aged, with graying black hair and wide brown eyes. Those eyes first went to him and then Gabrielle. She gripped on to the door as if she might slam it shut.

"It's okay," Gabrielle assured her, but her tone was

far from reassuring. "This is Houston Sadler. Houston, this is Lucas's nanny, Lily Rose Torres."

"Houston Sadler?" the woman repeated, with a gasp. "Why is he with you?"

"I had no choice but to bring him here," Gabrielle explained, in a whisper. "It's all right. Let him in." She moved past the nanny and into the room.

For a moment, Houston thought that Lily Rose might ignore Gabrielle's request and try to block him from entering, but the nanny finally stepped aside and locked the door once he was inside.

He walked into the room and glanced around. Two double beds divided by a nightstand, and a TV plopped onto an outdated dresser. There were baby clothes on one of the beds.

But no baby.

Houston was about to turn to Gabrielle and blast her for the deception, but then he heard the sound coming from the bathroom.

"I put Lucas in there when I heard someone knocking on the door," Lily Rose explained, and she headed in that direction.

The sound got a little louder, and it only took a few seconds before it turned until a full-fledged cry.

Definitely a baby.

That got Houston moving, and he trailed right along behind Lily Rose. Gabrielle did, too, but she pressed her forearm over her breasts.

"I have to nurse him," she mumbled. "My milk just let down."

Houston didn't have a clue what that last part meant,

but it was obvious that Gabrielle intended to breast-feed the baby.

Lily Rose stepped out of the tiny bathroom, holding an infant carrier in her right hand. Houston saw the movement then, the tiny kicks and squirms beneath the pale blue blanket.

"He's hungry," the nanny announced, grinning down at the baby. "I fed him a bottle about an hour ago, but I guess that wasn't enough for our growing boy." Still grinning, she brought the carrier toward Gabrielle.

And he got the first glimpse of his son's face.

It nearly brought Houston to his knees. *Oh, mercy.*

He'd seen pictures of himself as a baby, and Lucas was his spitting image. The dark brown hair, the shape of his face, that chin. He couldn't see the baby's eyes, but he was betting they were Sadler blue.

Houston had expected his first glimpse to pack a wallop, and it did. He looked into the carrier and saw that precious little face. It wasn't exactly one of those picture-perfect moments, because his son's face was flushed from crying, and it was obvious he wasn't happy. His sobs got even louder.

Gabrielle stepped in front of Houston and eased the baby from the carrier.

"It's all right," she murmured. "Mommy's here now."

She kissed the baby's cheek and carried him to one of the beds, where she sat and leaned back against the headboard. She smiled at Lucas. Really smiled.

Man.

It lit up her whole face. Gabrielle was a knockout,

even when she was glaring at him; but with that smile she was beautiful.

Houston shook his head to clear it. His brain was obviously turning to mush.

Gabrielle had already reached to pull up her top, but then her gaze came to his. "Uh, could you turn around?" she asked.

It wasn't an unreasonable request, but Houston hated to take his eyes off his son, even for a couple of minutes. He wanted nothing more than to reach out and take him. To kiss him the way Gabrielle had. He wanted to know what it felt like to hold that precious life in his hands.

But his son obviously preferred dinner.

Houston turned to the side and tried to keep his attention elsewhere. Still, the room was small, and he caught the movement from the corner of his eye when Gabrielle lifted her T-shirt. He also heard his son begin to nurse.

Houston had to take a deep breath.

Here he'd been so certain that he could just take Lucas and get custody of him, but the breast-feeding was a stark reminder that, while Lucas's DNA might be a match to Lizzy's, Gabrielle was the mommy he knew.

"I was worried about you," Lily Rose told Gabrielle, "so I checked for messages on the cell phone. I got your voicemail about you arriving at the Sadler ranch. There was also another message from your brother, Jay." She motioned to the notepad and the phone on the nightstand.

That got Houston's attention, and he looked at Gabrielle. Her top was still shoved up, but he couldn't see her breasts because Lucas was in front of them.

Gabrielle glanced at the notepad and then at Houston.

Before today, Jay was the only thing they had in common, and it wasn't a good connection to have. Houston figured any man who would abuse an animal wasn't someone he wanted within a hundred miles of his son.

"Jay calls you often?" Houston asked.

"Not really. Before I got pregnant, he hadn't spoken to me in months, but since the birth, he's called me nearly every day."

Houston didn't like the man's timing. "What does he want?"

"To see me, and Lucas," Gabrielle said, with a heavy sigh. "I told him I didn't have time to visit."

That was a massive understatement. But it got Houston thinking. "Is it possible Jay might have had something to do with those men in the black car?"

"No." But then she lifted her shoulder. "I don't think so, anyway."

It was yet something else that Houston needed to check out.

He glanced at the notepad on the nightstand. The nanny had written a phone number with the message: "Call your brother immediately. He says it's important."

Houston picked up the cell next to the note. "Why did Jay call you on this phone, rather than the one you had with you at the ranch?"

"Because that's the only number he has. It's the phone I used for business. I'm on maternity leave, but I still needed a way for the legal staff to contact me if a problem arose with one of my clients."

Houston cursed. "This cell can be traced."

"No. Both the ones I use are prepaid."

That caused him to relax a little, but that was only a drop in the bucket when it came to the safety measures he wanted to take.

Lily Rose picked up a purse from the dresser. "I think I'll go to the diner across the street and have a cup of coffee. Either of you want me to bring you back anything?"

"No," they said, in unison.

Lily Rose frowned at Gabrielle and headed for the door. "I'll get you a sandwich. With the way that boy's eating, you really need to get more food in you."

Houston welcomed the woman's concern, and the privacy she was about to give them. It was obvious Gabrielle and he were going to have to have a serious discussion. A discussion she wouldn't like.

He followed the nanny to the door and locked it after she left.

Gabrielle didn't look at him while she continued to nurse. She stared down at the baby and gently ran her fingers through his wispy hair. It was such a simple gesture, but it was intimate, too.

Houston wanted to be part of that.

"Did the gunmen who took you hostage touch Lucas or you?" Houston asked.

"No. They didn't have to. I cooperated. I just kept thinking that I would do whatever it took to get Lucas out of there safely."

Her fingers were still caressing the baby's hair, and she seemed almost serene sitting there; but Houston figured she was reliving the nightmare of that incident. He wished he'd been there to help.

But he hadn't even known his son existed at that time.

Gabrielle shifted a little, fixed her nursing bra and eased down her top. She placed the baby against her chest and shoulder so she could burp him.

Houston moved closer to get a better look…and soon realized he was smiling. It all became clear then. He understood why his friends got all sappy when they talked about their children.

He eased down on the bed across from them, reached out and touched Lucas's hair as Gabrielle had done. The baby stirred and turned his head, so that he was facing Houston.

"He's perfect," Houston heard himself say.

"Yes," Gabrielle agreed. "I've wanted a child for as long as I can remember."

So had he. But unlike him, Gabrielle had done something to make that happen. "You said something earlier about being infertile. What happened?" he asked.

She took a deep breath. "I had leukemia when I was thirteen, and the chemo left me unable to produce eggs of my own. I always knew I'd have children, and last year the time was right for a baby."

He was prying, but he wanted to know what had brought them to this point. "Why then?"

Another deep breath, but she didn't seem annoyed. She had her attention fastened to Lucas. "I was about to turn thirty-three—but I wasn't in a relationship. I hadn't been in one for a long time. Plus, I figured it might take years for me to get pregnant." She kissed the top of Lucas's head. "It didn't. It worked on the first try."

If it hadn't—if Gabrielle had used another

embryo—then they wouldn't be here together in this room. Lucas wouldn't exist.

Hell.

It was hard for Houston to stay furious with his father when he was looking at his son's face. But he couldn't let Mack get away scot-free, either. This was past mere interference in Houston's life. His father should have told them what was going on long before Lucas was born.

Lucas let out a loud burp, causing both Gabrielle and Houston to chuckle. Again, the moment seemed intimate. And right.

He couldn't take his eyes off Lucas, and the baby was staring at him now. He'd been right about the eye color. They were blue.

"I'd like to hold him now," Houston said, gently.

Her chin didn't stay defiant and steely. She got a panicked look in her eyes.

"I just want to hold him," he assured her.

Of course, coming from him, that was no assurance at all. Still, Houston went closer and held out his hands. The moments passed slowly, before she finally surrendered and placed the baby in his arms.

The punch was instant. The overwhelming feeling of love. The need to protect. All of that was rolled into one gigantic wallop that made it hard for him to breathe. *Man.*

He was a goner.

Too bad he didn't get to feel that miracle for very long.

His phone rang, and Houston shifted the baby in his arms so he could glance at the caller ID.

"It's Dale," he told Gabrielle, "I need to answer it."

She immediately took the baby from him, and Houston mentally cursed. This call could be important, critical to their safety, but at the moment, nothing seemed more critical than holding his child.

"The black car finally stopped," Dale said, the moment Houston answered.

Finally, some good news. Well, maybe. "Where?"

"At an apartment on the south side of town. Two men got out of the vehicle and knocked on one of the doors. When they didn't get an answer, they got back into the vehicle and continued driving around."

"You know who the men are?" Houston asked.

"Not yet. But one of the ranch hands used his phone to get a picture, and he sent it to your security specialist friend, Jordan Taylor. Jordan's running the photo through all the databases now."

Good.

That meant Houston would soon know the names of the morons, and he would go after them. This wouldn't be a case of showing mercy, either. They would pay and pay hard.

"Your friend also ran the address of the apartment where the two men knocked," Dale continued. "He was able to identify the occupant through utility records."

"And?" Houston prompted when Dale didn't continue. "Who lives there?"

Dale hesitated again. "Gabrielle's brother, Jay Markham."

Chapter Six

"My father's already left," Houston told Gabrielle, as he led her through the estate house at the Blue Springs ranch.

"Are you sure? He could be lying about that." Gabrielle wanted to be sure, because Mack had given her a huge reason to distrust him.

"I'm sure. He's taking a little vacation to our place on Padre Island."

A little vacation.

Gabrielle was too tired to smile, but it was humorous in a sick, twisted way. She'd heard the phone conversation Houston had had with his father, and Houston had demanded that Mack leave immediately and not return until all of this was settled. It hadn't been a request, and Houston had made it clear that he was beyond furious with the man's actions. Hardly a little vacation.

Maybe, just maybe, Mack would do as he was told.

Gabrielle was actually thankful for the bone-weary fatigue, because that and Lucas were probably the reasons she hadn't come completely unglued.

Too much was coming at her at once, and she couldn't think straight. However, Gabrielle didn't need to think to realize that what she was doing could be another massive mistake. But what was one more? She'd started out the day with a mistake by taking that unloaded gun out to the ranch so she could get so-called answers from Houston. Well, she'd gotten those answers.

And here she was again. Right back in the very place where she was under Houston's control. But she was also under his protection.

She kept Lucas snuggled in her arms while they went upstairs to the second floor. He'd slept during the entire drive from the hotel to the ranch—perhaps because the adult occupants of the car had been silent, except for Houston's quietly spoken phone conversations. Houston and she had argued briefly at the hotel, after he'd told her about the men in the black car getting out at her brother's apartment.

It was a mistake, she'd tried to tell herself.

Her brother wouldn't endanger her.

But she had enough niggling doubt in the back of her mind that, when Houston insisted they all go to the ranch where he could keep Lucas safe, Gabrielle had only mildly resisted.

Truth was, Houston might be the only person who could protect Lucas. Gabrielle certainly wasn't going to rely on the police. The way Mack Sadler bought people off, he could buy off the cops, as well. They could take Lucas from her, claiming she was part of the coverup at the Cryogen Clinic, and it would be a long legal battle to get him back. Houston could prevent his father's further interference.

Probably.

But she wasn't stupid. Gabrielle had seen the love in

Houston's eyes when he looked at Lucas, and that love might blind him to fact that this was the child she'd planned and carried. This was *her* baby.

"Lily Rose, you can stay here," Houston said, opening one of the doors that lined the massive corridor. He set the nanny's suitcase just inside the guest room. "Gabrielle, you're next door."

He opened that room, as well, and it was even larger than she'd expected. A fourposter bed, a desk and even a sitting area. Decorated in varying shades of pales—blue, white and gray, it was tasteful and serene.

It included a crib and a changing table, which had been positioned against the right interior wall.

"I had the maid bring in some things," Houston explained. He placed her suitcase and the diaper bag on the floor next to the adjoining bathroom. "And there are some extra diapers and baby clothes."

Gabrielle had heard him make the request on the phone after the conversation with his father. After that, he had called Sheriff Whitley to tell him that he'd spoken with her, and that she had done nothing wrong at the Cryogen Clinic. However, Houston had added that he personally wanted to speak to the clinic head, because there had possibly been a coverup of some kind. However, Houston hadn't mentioned his father when he spoke of that coverup.

His next call had been to his security specialist friend, and Houston had asked him to check on Jay and on SAPD's investigation into the hostage situation. He was trying to determine if those hostage-taking gunmen did have an accomplice. An accomplice who might have been in that ominous black car that had stopped at Jay's apartment.

Houston had gotten several updates on that situation, as well, on the drive over. The two men had indeed knocked on Jay's door, but her brother hadn't answered. And according to the last update, the men were still driving around on the south side of San Antonio.

Gabrielle looked around the room and spotted the diapers and clothes that Houston had mentioned. They were stacked on the changing table. "The maid didn't have much time to set all of this up," she commented. Houston had made that request less than an hour earlier.

He shrugged. "We keep cribs and baby items for guests. We have extra clothes and toiletries for Lily Rose and you, too, if you need them."

"We brought our own things," Gabrielle told him, and she frowned at the iciness in her voice. She really wanted to blame Houston for all of this, but it seemed less and less likely that he'd had any part in it.

"I'm going to freshen up," Lily Rose said. "If you need me, just give a yell."

The woman glanced at Gabrielle, probably to see if she had any objections to being left alone with Houston. She did. But Lily Rose didn't need to babysit her.

"It's okay," Gabrielle assured her, and Lily Rose went off to her room.

"You're exhausted," Houston commented.

And as if it was the most normal and routine thing in the world, he took Lucas from her arms and carried him to the crib. He didn't lay the baby down right away, but instead kissed his cheek and smiled at him.

Gabrielle could see it then—the strong resemblance.

It was uncanny and unnerving just how much Lucas looked like his father. He was indeed a Sadler.

That didn't do much to steady her nerves.

Houston glanced back at her and his smile faded. Heaven knows how horrible and terrified she must have looked, because it prompted him to lay the baby down on his side in the crib. Houston tucked the blanket around Lucas and came back across the room toward her.

"You look like you're ready to pass out. Or something. It's almost dinnertime," he said, checking his watch. "I can have trays brought up for Lily Rose and you."

"Thank you." And she meant it. She was too numb to be hungry, but she had to eat for Lucas's sake.

Houston stared at her. "About Jay…" However, he ended that with a heavy, frustrated breath.

"I'll talk to him," Gabrielle insisted, "but I'm sure there's a reasonable explanation for why those men went to his apartment. It's probably just some kind of mix-up. Jay hasn't lived there very long, so maybe the guys were looking for the previous owner."

Though that did seem like a strange coincidence.

"You're defending him again." Houston didn't say that with anger, or even as an accusation. Merely as a statement of fact.

It was true. She was indeed defending Jay, something she'd done most of her life. "He's my kid brother," Gabrielle settled for saying.

"And you practically raised him after your mother was killed when you were nineteen," Houston added.

She blinked, surprised that he knew that about her.

Houston just shrugged. "I had a background check run on you when Jay brought the lawsuit against me."

Of course he had; and he probably knew that Jay had been in and out of trouble since he was fourteen. Their mother's death had sent him into a bad spiral that had led to a lot of bad choices—and a juvenile arrest record for drug possession. Since their father had left years earlier, when Jay was just a baby, Gabrielle had taken care of him out of necessity.

"I didn't do a good job of raising him," Gabrielle mumbled.

"You were nineteen," Houston countered. He took her by the arm and led her to the love seat in the sitting area. "Sit down," he insisted.

She did, because she wasn't sure she could stand much longer anyway. Houston sat next to her.

"You're having an adrenaline crash," he explained. "If you want to take a nap, I can sit here and watch the baby while you sleep."

It was so tempting, but the reprieve wouldn't be without consequences. She should be trying to push Houston away and not draw him closer into their lives.

Like now, for instance.

Unlike the rest of the room and the house, the love seat wasn't that large, and Houston and she were practically hip to hip. Much too close.

"Right," he mumbled, as if he knew exactly what she was thinking. And feeling.

Houston slowly got to his feet and began to make his way to the door. He didn't get even halfway when his phone rang. The noise shot through the room, and Lucas immediately began to cry.

She hurried to the crib. So did Houston. But he stopped when he saw the number on his caller ID screen.

He gave her a glance to let her know it was important, and Gabrielle picked up the baby while Houston took the call.

"Sheriff Whitley, what can I do for you?" Houston walked to the doorway and just into the hall, probably because Lucas launched into a full-fledged cry.

Gabrielle put the baby against her chest and gently rocked him. Lucas crammed his fist into his mouth and began to suck. That, and the rocking, soothed him almost immediately.

Houston's call was one-sided, because he didn't say a word for several long moments. And as each one passed, Gabrielle began to imagine the worst. Had the men in that car gotten away from the ranch hands? Were they on their way to the ranch for a fresh attack?

"Could you send that picture to my cell phone?" Houston asked. "Salvador Franks, that's right," he added, a moment later.

That got her attention. Salvador Franks was the head of the Cryogen Clinic, and if Mack had told the truth, he was the one who was responsible for the mix-up with the embryo.

"Well, I want to talk to him, too." Houston looked back at her. "No, I'd rather not go into town right now. I'm tied up here at the ranch." He paused. "That'll be fine. I'm anxious to talk to him."

Houston ended the call and made his way back to her. He gave Lucas a rub on the cheek before his gaze came to hers. "The sheriff's on the way out here, and he has Salvador Franks with him."

Gabrielle stopped the rocking, but Lucas's whimpers

had her starting right back up again. "Already? You only called him about Cryogen an hour ago."

"Sheriff Whitley works fast, and he wants to help. Don't worry, though, I won't let Salvador near you or Lucas."

She shook her head. "But I want to hear what he has to say about what happened at the clinic and about his conversation with your father."

"That might not be a good idea. There are things going on, and I don't know just how involved this Salvador Franks is."

Before she could ask what he meant by that, Houston held up his phone, and she saw the photo of the man. He was in his late thirties or early forties and had dark hair.

"Who is he?" she wanted to know.

"Harlan Cordell. He's a shady businessman and occasional loan shark. SAPD believes he might be the accomplice to the gunmen who held the maternity hospital hostage."

Gabrielle's heart dropped. So it was true. There really *was* an accomplice. *Oh, mercy.*

Was this the man who'd made her life hell for the past six weeks? Or was Mack to blame for that?

She shifted Lucas so she could get a better look at the small photo. She studied Harlan Cordell's face but finally had to shake her head. "I don't recognize him. Why does SAPD think he's involved?"

"An undercover officer learned that the two dead gunmen owed Cordell a lot of money. Word on the street is that Cordell went to the hospital the day of the hostage situation to assist the gunmen who were getting paid to destroy some lab files. Cordell probably wanted to make sure their pay went to him."

Gabrielle had followed the investigation in the papers, and it was true. One of the dying gunmen had confessed that they owed money and were little more than hired guns for someone who had offered them lots of money to destroy evidence in the hospital lab. But the man who'd hired the gunmen had also been arrested and was awaiting trial.

"Look at the picture again," Houston said, pressing her.

She did, but after a few seconds, she knew her answer would be the same. "I don't think I've ever seen him."

"Word on the street says otherwise."

Her breath stalled in her chest. "What do you mean?"

"According to the undercover officer, Cordell thinks you saw him with the gunmen that day in the hospital when you were taken hostage."

Gabrielle shook her head so hard that Lucas stirred and started to fuss again. "Is that why he's been following me?" she asked. "Is that why he tried to run us off the road today?"

Houston eased both Lucas and her into his arms. "I'm not sure. Neither is SAPD. But it could be that Cordell is trying to intimidate you so there's no chance you'll testify against him."

When her lungs began to ache, she had no choice but to release the breath she'd been holding. "I was right. Lucas and I are in danger."

"You were. But you're safe now. I intend to get to the bottom of this."

Gabrielle wanted to believe him, but if the police hadn't been able to arrest Harlan Cordell, then it might not be easy for Houston to stop him, either. Of course, Houston and she had Lucas to protect, and that was a more powerful motive than others' needs of eliminating her as a potential witness.

Because Lucas had fallen back asleep and because her arms suddenly felt like pudding, Gabrielle placed him back in the crib. Houston joined her, stood right by her side, and together they stared down at the baby.

"Thank you," she heard him say.

Gabrielle risked looking at him and saw the fatigue mirrored in his eyes. She also saw the emotion. "For what?"

He didn't answer right away, and it seemed as if he changed his mind several times about what he was about to say. "For giving birth to Lucas."

She pulled back her shoulders and was ready to tell him she didn't want his thanks. But before Gabrielle could get out a syllable, Houston slid his arm around her and pulled her to him. She automatically started to push him away, but something stopped her. Maybe it was the adrenaline crash. Or the fatigue. Or the uncertainty of what she was going to do about their safety. Whichever it was, Gabrielle found herself leaning into him and drawing comfort from the very man she should be avoiding.

"This isn't a good idea," she mumbled.

"No. It's not." But neither of them moved.

"We have so much to work out between us, and *this* can't get in the way," Gabrielle said, trying again.

He didn't question what *this* was, and that meant he was feeling the attraction, too.

"Maybe it'll go away," she added.

He made a sound deep within his chest to let her know he didn't buy that. Neither did she. But just because there was an attraction, it didn't mean they had to act on it.

Gabrielle forced herself away from him. It wasn't as good an idea as she thought it would be. Again, Houston and she were face-to-face. And very close. So close that she could see all those swirls of blue in his eyes. Close enough for her to take in his scent. The man was drop-dead hot, and those looks and that smell pulled her right in.

"When the sheriff gets here, I'll tell him about my father's involvement with Salvador Franks," Houston explained. "I want a thorough investigation into what happened at the Cryogen Clinic. If there was a cover-up, or if my father bribed someone, I want that all out in the open. Because what he did to you was wrong. He should have come clean about the baby you were carrying, and he shouldn't have followed you the way he did."

That stunned her almost as much as the ill-timed attraction. "Your father could go to jail," she reminded him.

Because they were so close, she saw that realization register in his eyes. Not surprise, but pain. "I know, but I can't let him get away with this."

Gabrielle studied his face to make sure he wasn't giving her lip service. He wasn't. A deeply troubled face stared back at her.

Oh, this wasn't good. Attraction and now empathy. It

was a volatile mix, especially when combined with the dangerous situation they'd gone through together.

Gabrielle stood and made a vague motion toward the door. "Uh, you should go."

"Yeah," he readily agreed, "I should." Houston glanced at Lucas again. "For the next hour or so, I'll be in my office, at the end of the hall and to the right. And if I'm not there, I'll probably be in my bedroom. It's just door next to yours."

"Next door," she repeated. That was a little too close for comfort, but then the entire estate suddenly didn't seem big enough for both of them.

"When Lucas wakes up, I'd like to know," he said. "I'd like to hold him again."

Gabrielle managed a nod, though part of her wanted to say no. She cursed this miserable attraction and the danger. Both were tearing down barriers that were better left in place.

"Is there anything you need?" he asked.

She didn't need him to hold her again, but it had certainly felt good. Too good. And that's why it couldn't happen again.

It did, though.

Sort of. Houston didn't pull her back to him, but he did touch her arm, and rubbed gently.

There was a knock, and Houston and she flew apart as if they'd been caught doing something they shouldn't have been doing. Which wasn't far from the truth.

Gabrielle looked in the doorway, and there stood Dale, Houston's ranch foreman. The man seemed surprised, probably because of the arm touching he'd just witnessed.

"Sorry to interrupt," Dale said, "but we got a problem." He was holding a piece of paper between his thumb and forefinger as if it were a fragile piece of crystal.

"Are Salvador Franks and the sheriff here yet?" Houston asked.

"No, but I'm expecting them any minute. Our unexpected visitor is her brother, Jay," Dale said to Houston.

Both Houston and she froze.

"He just arrived at the ranch," Dale explained. "And he wants to see Gabrielle."

"Jay's at the ranch?" Gabrielle questioned.

"Yeah. I had him wait in the sitting room. When the sheriff gets here, he's taking Salvador Franks to the back den. I didn't know if you wanted all of them in the same room or not."

Gabrielle shook her head. "How did Jay even know I was here?"

Dale's mouth tightened. "He wouldn't say."

"Maybe not to you." Houston started for the door. "But he'll sure as hell tell me."

Dale stepped in front of him. "There's more." He handed Houston the paper he'd brought with him. "The security specialist was finally able to get an ID on the two men in that black car."

Houston looked at what Dale had given him and cursed. He wadded up the paper and stormed out of the room.

Chapter Seven

Houston had thought this day couldn't possibly get any more complicated, but it apparently had.

He started for the stairs, but then realized Gabrielle was right behind him. He knew for a fact he didn't want her at this meeting with her brother, but he doubted he could stop her. Besides, she had a right to be there.

Especially after what Houston had just learned.

He crushed the paper in his fist into an even tighter ball, and considered ripping it to pieces. It wouldn't help. It damn sure wouldn't undo things, but it might soothe his temper before he faced Jay Markham.

"Wait for me," Gabrielle insisted.

She knocked on the nanny's door, and the moment Lily Rose answered, Gabrielle handed her the baby. "I need you to watch Lucas. My brother's here. And something's apparently wrong."

There was no *apparently* to it. Something *was* wrong. And Houston was about to make whatever it was right, even if he had to beat the truth out of Jay.

"Wait up here," Houston instructed Dale. "Make sure Lucas stays safe."

Not that Houston expected a break-in, or for Jay to

try to storm upstairs and kidnap the baby. He'd activated the house's security system, but with all the coming and going, it wasn't foolproof.

Gabrielle caught up with him at the bottom of the stairs. "What did Dale give you?" she asked.

Houston was about to tell her, if he could get his teeth unclenched, that is, but he looked through the arched doorway of the nearby sitting room and saw Jay standing there, watching them.

Jay hadn't changed much since he'd worked at the ranch. He still had the beefy build and shaggy blond hair that was an almost identical color to his sister's. He had a genetic copy of her eyes, as well.

But that's where the similarities ended.

Gabrielle was nothing like her brother. Houston knew that now. And he didn't think his change of heart had anything to do with the fact that she'd given birth to his son.

"Houston Sadler," Jay spat out, like profanity.

"Jay Markham." Houston returned the tone, and he tossed the wadded up paper onto the foyer table. "What are you doing here?"

Jay looked past Houston and at Gabrielle. Even though he didn't say her name, the profanity was still there in his expression.

"I'm here to see my sister," Jay said. He aimed a glare at Gabrielle.

Houston had several questions for her brother, but he went with the first on his list. "How did you know she was here?"

He turned that glare on Houston. "A friend of a friend told me."

"That's not a good enough answer. Someone tried to hurt Gabrielle today. Call me testy, but I want to know the identity of this friend of a friend."

Jay's glare softened a bit, and he looked at Gabrielle as if he wanted her to verify what Houston had just said.

She nodded. "Someone tried to run us off the road. And then that someone went to your apartment."

Jay had already opened his mouth when Gabrielle finished the first sentence. But the second sentence had his eyes widening. He volleyed glances between Houston and her and then cursed.

"You don't think I had anything to do with trying to hurt you, do you?" Jay demanded.

"I don't know," Gabrielle said.

"I believe you did," Houston disagreed. "So who told you that she was here?"

Jay made more of those volleying glances, and his breathing sped up. He groaned and leaned against the doorway.

"A couple of days ago, I got a visit from someone I owe money. I couldn't make the payment he wanted, so he said I could work off part of the loan if I gave him some information." Jay looked at Gabrielle. "He wanted to know where you were."

Gabrielle's hand flew to her chest, and she covered her heart with her palm. "Who is this man?"

"I didn't tell him anything," Jay said, avoiding her question. "Because I didn't know where you were. Then, this afternoon, he calls again and says you're out here at the Sadler ranch. I didn't believe him. I thought this was the last place on earth you'd go." The glare returned.

"Obviously I was wrong. What? Are you sleeping with Houston Sadler now?"

Houston heard Gabrielle's low sound of outrage, but he didn't know how. It was hard to hear anything over the sudden pounding in his ears.

He grabbed on to Jay and slammed him against the wall. "Who told you Gabrielle was here?"

Jay grimaced, but he kept his eyes narrowed and defiant. "I only know him as Lanny."

"Lanny," Houston repeated. He glanced back at Gabrielle. "Otherwise known as Harlan Cordell. The man in the black car, who stopped at Jay's apartment."

"What?" Gabrielle's voice was more breath than sound, and she walked toward them, with her gaze fastened on her brother. "Harlan Cordell told you where I was?"

"If that's his real name, yeah, he's the one who told me. Why? And after you answer that little question, sis, you can tell me why you're here with the likes of him." Jay fought to get out of his Houston's grip. But Houston just slammed him harder against the wall.

Gabrielle came closer, until she was shoulder-to-shoulder with Houston, and she got right in her brother's face. "The cops believe Harlan Cordell was an accomplice of the men who took me and the other women hostage last month at the maternity hospital. But they don't have enough proof to arrest him."

Houston studied Jay's reaction. He seemed to be genuinely surprised at that revelation, but Houston figured it could all be an act. He didn't trust anyone who would abuse an animal and talk to his sister the way Jay just had.

"What exactly did Cordell say about Gabrielle?" Houston demanded.

"He wanted me to call her and arrange a meeting. Lanny said it was important, that she might be in some kind of trouble. Trouble that he could fix for her."

"And in turn, he could fix the loan for you." Houston cursed again. "Didn't you get suspicious about a loan shark wanting to help your sister?"

"No. Lanny seems like a man with connections, and I thought maybe Gabrielle and he were friends or something. I thought she wouldn't mind helping me out a little. All she'd have to do is meet with Lanny, and it would save my butt, along with a lot of money."

"He's definitely not a friend, and I'm not meeting with him," Gabrielle mumbled. She groaned and pushed her hair away from her face. "How did Harlan Cordell even know I was here at the ranch?"

Jay shook his head. "I don't know. That's the truth!" he practically shouted, when Houston gave him another slam against the wall.

Houston released the grip he had on him, but he stayed close. "Here's what you're going to do," Houston started. "You'll contact Cordell and find out what he wants with Gabrielle."

Jay looked ready to defy that order, but then he glanced at Gabrielle. Maybe, just maybe, there was enough brotherly concern for him to do the right thing. "Okay."

"You'll call me when you hear from Cordell," Houston continued. "But you won't come back here to the ranch. If you do, I'll have you arrested for trespassing. Understand?"

"Yeah. I understand." His teeth came together, and he aimed another of those venomous looks at Houston. "I also understand that Gabrielle is stupid to come to you for help."

Houston was about to latch on to the man again, but Gabrielle beat him to it. She grabbed Jay by the arm. "You might be my kid brother, but I'm fed up with this conversation. You're leaving now."

Jay froze and stared at her as if stunned that she would side with Houston on this. Probably because Gabrielle had spent a lifetime defending him. "You're choosing Houston Sadler over me?"

"For the time being, yes." The grip she had on Jay melted away. "As far as I can tell, Houston isn't trying to set me up in a meeting with a man who might want me dead."

"No, but he might be trying to do far worse."

Houston wanted to know what Jay meant by that, but he heard the footsteps. Greta, one of the maids, was making her way up the east corridor toward them.

"Sheriff Whitley just arrived," Greta let him know. "He's in the den, and he has a guest with him."

That guest was Salvador Franks, yet someone else who might have some pieces to this puzzle. Houston figured Jay had more pieces, as well, but he doubted he'd get the truth out of him. Right now, the safest thing he could do for Gabrielle and Lucas was to get Jay off the ranch.

Houston grabbed on to Jay again and led him to the front door. Jay didn't exactly put up a fight about leaving, but he did look back at Gabrielle.

"Rethink this," Jay warned her. "Don't cast your lot with the Sadlers."

"You haven't given me any reason to cast my lot with you," she fired back.

Though Gabrielle sounded convinced about that, Houston still saw the pain her eyes. This break with her brother was costing her big-time. Even though Jay couldn't be trusted, that didn't mean she didn't still love him. This had to be hell for her.

Jay threw off Houston's grip when he went onto the porch, but he spun around to face Gabrielle again. "You need to speak to Lanny, or as you call him, Harlan Cordell. I'm sure he has some very interesting information that you need to hear."

Gabrielle folded her arms over her chest. "What do you mean?"

Jay didn't answer right away. Then he glanced at Houston and flashed an oily smile. The man didn't say another word until he reached his car.

"Sis, you really want to know how Cordell knew you were here at the ranch?" He didn't wait for her to confirm that. "Just ask Houston's father. I'm sure he can tell you all about it."

GABRIELLE STARTED TO GO after her brother, but Houston stopped her.

"He's lying," Houston told her. "Jay just wants to get a rise out of you."

It had worked. But in addition to making her even angrier, her brother also given her yet another reason to be concerned.

"I don't want Jay trying to pull you into the car with him," Houston added.

That stopped her. Because it was indeed something Jay might do. If he truly thought she was making a mistake by being here at the ranch, he might try to take her against her will. If that happened, Lucas would be left behind. She wasn't leaving her baby for any reason, especially not for her brother's suspicions.

"What if he's not lying about your father?" she asked, as Houston led her back inside. She looked over her shoulder as Jay drove away.

"Then we'll deal with it." Houston stopped in the foyer and relocked the door. He also set the security system from a small panel on the wall.

Gabrielle shook her head and tried again. "Could your father have really been the one to tell Harlan Cordell I was here?"

Houston looked as if he wanted to deny that, but he, too, shook his head. "Just as you want to trust Jay, I want to trust my dad. But I can't. That's why he's not here right now. And that's why I don't want him here until we can figure out what's going on."

He caught on to her shoulders and made eye contact. "We're on the same side here, Gabrielle."

They were. How ironic. Twenty-four hours ago, they'd been old enemies, and now Houston was the only person who had as much to lose as she did.

Lucas was their bond. For now.

Soon, hopefully very soon, the danger would be resolved. Cordell and anyone who'd assisted him would be behind bars, and then Houston and she could go onto the next battle: custody of Lucas.

"Why don't you skip this meeting with Salvador Franks?" Houston suggested. "You must be exhausted."

She was, and it wouldn't be long before she would need to feed Lucas again. Still, she wanted to hear what the head of the Cryogen Clinic had to say about what had happened to her.

"I'm going with you," she insisted.

Houston stared at her as if he might put up an argument, but he nodded and slipped his arm around her waist. They made their way down the corridor together. Apparently, the sheriff and his visitor had come in through the rear door, because the den was the last room at the east end of the estate.

Gabrielle saw Sheriff Whitley standing in front of the massive fireplace that took up a good one-third of the wall. His guest had thick black hair and a moustache, and he was seated on a burgundy leather sofa. He had a briefcase clutched in his right hand.

Salvador Franks, no doubt.

Gabrielle thought she might recognize him, but she didn't. When she'd filled out an application for a donor embryo, she'd dealt with the intake counselor, and then the doctor, who'd actually performed the procedure.

"Sheriff," Houston said his greeting with a nod. Then he turned his attention to Salvador, who got to his feet.

Unlike her brother, there was no defiance in Salvador's nearly black eyes or his posture. Every muscle in his body seemed to be tensed, and there was perspiration above his upper lip.

"Ms. Markham," he said to her. He put his briefcase aside and shook hands with Houston. "Mr. Sadler. Sheriff Whitley said you had some questions for me."

Houston motioned for her to sit on the matching sofa that was directly across from their visitor, and Gabrielle did. After the encounter with her brother, she didn't feel too steady on her feet.

"I suppose I should start by asking if I need to call my attorney," Salvador said.

She glanced at Houston, and he shook his head. "We only want answers," Gabrielle explained. "However, if there are charges brought against the Cryogen Clinic or some member of your staff, you have my word that I won't use anything you say here against you."

Salvador stared at her, obviously considering that. "All right. What do you want to know?"

"Tell us what happened when Gabrielle came to Cryogen," Houston said.

Salvador sat down. He nodded, swallowed hard and then nodded again. "About eleven months ago, Ms. Markham completed the application and had a routine exam. She was approved. Unfortunately, during the actual in vitro procedure, there was a mix-up. She was given the wrong embryo."

"One that belonged to my late wife and me," Houston reminded him.

The man bobbed his head. "It was a clerical mix-up. The intake counselor put the wrong code on Ms. Markham's medical chart."

Gabrielle jumped right on that. "And you think that was an accident?"

"Of course." He opened his mouth, closed it, and then

his eyes widened. "You don't believe we gave you the wrong embryo on purpose?"

"You tell me," she countered.

"It was a simple mistake," Salvador insisted. He repeated that, turning his gaze first to Houston and then the sheriff. "There was no malice involved."

"Maybe not malice," Houston stated, "but there was a cover-up."

"No," the man insisted. He gave his tie an adjustment it didn't need. "Not on my part, anyway. Nor on the part of the clinic. When I realized that Ms. Markham had been given the wrong embryo, I called you immediately. I explained what had happened."

"But you didn't talk to me," Houston clarified. "You talked to my father."

"Only because he claimed to be you. He lied, pure and simple. And he continued to lie when he came to the clinic."

"And you didn't notice that a man claiming to be me was more than twenty years older than I am?" Houston pressed.

Salvador shook his head. "I didn't even notice the birth year on the original records. By then, I was more concerned about getting a signature for the embryo's use."

Salvador reached into his briefcase and took out a piece of paper. It was some kind of form. "That's the agreement your father signed."

"What kind of agreement?" Houston wanted to know.

"Postdated approval for use of the embryo. It absolves

us of any legal action. Or it should. We had no idea your father was pretending to be you."

Gabrielle took the paper and saw that it did indeed have Houston's signature. The signature his father had no doubt forged. But it wasn't the signature that concerned her. It was Mack's actions afterward.

"When you realized I'd been given the wrong embryo, did it occur to you to tell me? Or, by then, had Mack Sadler agreed to pay you to keep this from me?"

"No." But he didn't seem nearly as assured as he had been just seconds earlier. He gave his tie another wiggle, pinching it to his throat. "Mr. Sadler and I discussed the possibility of telling you, but we decided there was no reason. You'd asked for a donor embryo. In fact, it would have been a violation of the clinic rules to provide you with the identities of the donors. We keep that confidential, unless all parties have agreed in advance."

"But I was given an embryo that didn't have the proper approval to be donated," Gabrielle pointed out.

"True. But there was no reason for you to know that. I did an internal investigation and reprimanded the intake counselor for the mistake. There are no more of your embryos, so I assure you this can't happen again. And with the new security measures I've put in place, it won't happen to anyone else, either."

Houston moved to the edge of the sofa so he could meet the man eye to eye. "Did my father bribe you, or did he pressure you to use that specific embryo?"

Salvador got to his feet again, and he reached out and took the authorization form from her. "No."

That didn't seem like a lie, exactly, but Gabrielle had no doubt that Mack had pressured this man into staying quiet. And then Mack had followed her with the intention of trying to buy Lucas from her. Still, she wasn't sure an actual crime had been committed, other than Mack impersonating his son and forging his name.

At a minimum, Mack had committed fraud and forgery, and there were possibly some other charges dealing with impersonation. But she would leave that for Houston to deal with. Right now she had her own issues to sort out with her brother, and she was too bone tired to think straight.

She stood. "If you'll excuse me, I need to check on my son." She turned to the sheriff. "Thank you for bringing Mr. Franks out here to talk with us."

Houston stood, as well, added his thanks to hers and began to escort Salvador and the sheriff toward the door. However, they didn't get far before the sheriff's phone buzzed. Gabrielle didn't wait; she started for her room. She really just needed to hold Lucas and make sure he was okay. The events of the day were starting to close in on her.

"Harlan Cordell," she heard the sheriff say to the caller.

That stopped her in her tracks, and Gabrielle quickly made her way back to the others so she could find out what had prompted Sheriff Whitley to mention the man's name. The man who was perhaps an accomplice of the gunmen who'd held the maternity hostages.

Houston had stopped, as well, even though Salvador was already on his way out the door. Gabrielle was actually thankful for that because, judging from the sheriff's suddenly alarmed expression, this was not going to be good news, and they didn't need an audience for it.

"What's wrong?" Houston asked the moment the sheriff ended the call.

"One of the deputies spotted Harlan Cordell at a convenience store about ten minutes ago, and he tried to stop him so he could bring him in for questioning. Cordell jumped in his car and sped away."

Houston cursed. "Is the deputy in pursuit?"

The sheriff shook his head. "No, he lost him. He thinks maybe Cordell turned onto one of the side roads and parked out of sight."

Sheriff Whitley glanced at Gabrielle before staring at Houston. "My advice? Lock up tight for the night, because according to the deputy, the last he saw of Cordell, he was heading in this direction."

Chapter Eight

Houston gave the breakfast tray an adjustment so he could knock on Gabrielle's door. He kept the knock light, just in case she and Lucas were still sleeping. Part of him hoped they were, but that hope went south when Gabrielle threw open the door almost immediately.

She was dressed in dark jeans and a blue top, and since her hair was wet, he figured she hadn't just gotten out of bed but rather the shower. Her eyes were sleep starved, and there were dark circles beneath. Still, she managed to look incredible.

Something he tried not to notice.

And failed.

And he stood there, probably looking dumb-founded.

"Anything from the sheriff on Cordell?" she whispered.

"No. I've been getting updates from him all night, and as of about an hour ago, the deputies were still combing the area looking for him."

She made a soft, frustrated-sounding sigh. Something Houston totally understood. This whole situation with

Cordell and her brother, Jay, wasn't just frustrating, it was potentially dangerous.

"I thought you might be hungry," Houston said.

He tipped his head to the tray that the cook had assembled. There were scrambled eggs, bacon and toast beneath a glass dome cover, and she'd also added a cup of coffee and some orange juice.

She stepped to the side so that Houston could bring the food inside. He set it on the table in the sitting area and then peeked over at a sleeping Lucas. Houston felt the punch again. The love. And he wondered if he would feel that way every time he looked at his son.

"I can't drink coffee," Gabrielle said softly. "Caffeine and breast feeding don't mix, but everything else looks delicious. Thank you."

She helped herself to a piece of a toast, but Houston didn't think it was his imagination that she was eating out of necessity, and not because she was actually hungry.

"I heard Lucas wake up around 1:00 a.m.," Houston commented. He sank down onto the love seat next to her. "And again at five." It had taken every ounce of his willpower not to come into the room and join Gabrielle and the baby, but Houston had known she'd be nursing Lucas and that she wouldn't have wanted an audience for it.

"Yes. Sorry he woke you."

"No need to apologize. It was…" He gave a nervous, low laugh. "Maybe because this is all still so new to me, I'd hoped he would wake up more often. I like to hear him, even if he's fussing."

She didn't refute that, and the corner of her mouth lifted just slightly. "Then you're in luck. You'll hear a lot of waking and fussing. He usually wants to nurse about every four hours." Gabrielle looked at the clock. It was just past eight, which meant he would be waking up again in about an hour. "Lily Rose came over and watched him while I showered, but then I sent her back to bed. She didn't sleep well."

Houston figured that was true for all them. Well, except for Lucas. Thank God the baby was too young to understand what was happening.

She finished the toast and had several bites of the scrambled eggs while Houston drank the coffee. Both of them continued to glance back at the crib—probably to avoid looking at each other.

But it happened anyway. Their gazes collided and froze.

"I had some time to think last night," Gabrielle said. "And it isn't a good idea for us to be here."

"Us? As in Lucas and you?"

She nodded, looked away again. Gabrielle set the orange juice back on the tray. "I'll hire a bodyguard to keep us safe, but I can't stay here."

Houston leaned forward and set the coffee cup next to her juice. "Because of what Jay said about my father?"

"That's part of it." She slipped her fingers through her damp, blond hair to push it away from her forehead. It was such a simple gesture, but one that struck him as completely feminine.

Houston silently groaned and got his mind back on the conversation.

"Jay insinuated that your father might have been the one to tell Cordell that I was at the ranch. I don't believe that," she quickly added, "but I do believe your father doesn't have my best interest at heart."

"He doesn't," Houston readily agreed. "And that's why he's not here. I own this ranch, Gabrielle. I bought out my father's part in it three years ago, when he wanted to make other investments."

"But he's your father. This is his home," she pointed out. "He'll want to return."

"That won't happen, unless I'm certain he won't make trouble for you."

Now her gaze came back to his. "*You* could make trouble for me."

So they were on the subject of custody. He hoped. Better than talking about the attraction. "I could. You could make trouble for me, too. Or we could try to work out something together that doesn't involve making trouble."

"What do you mean? Are you talking about split custody?" A flash of anger went through her eyes. "Because I don't want that for my son. The reason I used what I thought was a donor embryo, was so I wouldn't have these custody questions. I didn't want to share him with anyone."

"I know. I can't go back and undo what happened at the clinic. And even if could, I wouldn't. Because the result of that mix-up is Lucas."

She blinked hard, as if fighting tears, and she probably was. Her emotions had to be running sky-high. His certainly were.

Houston considered trying to reassure her that he would be fair when it came to a custody arrangement, but in Gabrielle's mind, the only fair thing would be for his father and him to disappear from Lucas's life.

That wasn't going to happen.

For him to be part of Lucas's future, he would have to encroach on the future that Gabrielle had so carefully planned for herself.

"I'm sorry," Houston settled for saying.

She blinked back more tears, and even though Houston knew this would be a massive mistake, he pulled her into his arms.

Yeah, it was a mistake, all right.

Gabrielle seemed to melt right into him.

He felt a punch of a different kind, but still a familiar one. That damn attraction reared its head, and it didn't take much of the embrace for his stupid body to start making all kinds of stupid suggestions.

Like a kiss, for instance. What harm could it do?

Houston was trying hard to talk himself out of doing just that, but then he felt his head lower anyway. Gabrielle looked up at him, probably to scold him for thinking such a thing.

But Houston kissed her anyway.

She smelled like strawberry shampoo and tasted like oranges, but that wasn't the first thing about her that registered in Houston's mind. The first thing he noticed was that the taste of her went straight through him, heating his entire body with just the touch of her mouth.

Of course, he didn't keep it a touch.

When Gabrielle didn't resist, Houston pulled her even closer to him, angled her head and deepened what he had started.

So, what harm could it do?

Plenty.

Kissing Gabrielle was a mistake, but French kissing her pushed him into the dumb-as-dirt arena.

He gathered his wherewithal so he could end this, but then Gabrielle played dirty. She made a sound of sweet feminine pleasure, and she lifted her arms. First one. Then, the other. And she eased them around his neck.

Oh, man. This wasn't stopping.

Since the mistake was already out there, Houston decided to make it worth it. He slid his hand down her back, inching even closer, until they were pressed right against each other. It was a good fit, with her breasts against his chest. He could feel her hardened and puckered nipples, and her fingers, as they trailed lightly down his neck.

The fire went white-hot.

He wanted her. Not just for this kiss, either. Houston wanted all of her, and even though his brain was telling him why that couldn't happen, the kiss was overriding anything left of his common sense.

Gabrielle finally broke the mouth-to-mouth contact, and gasping for air, stared at him—for just a couple of seconds—before she dove back in for what was apparently about to be round two.

This time, she kissed him.

Not that Houston needed it, but that was confirmation that this attraction was far from one-sided. It also confirmed that it wasn't cooling anytime soon.

He slid his hand lower, just to the top of her butt, and he shifted his position so that he could bring them even closer. Yet another stupid idea. They were already too close, but with some maneuvering, he pulled her onto his lap.

She gasped, and he caught the surprised sound in his own mouth, and looked between them. There was no space. They were pressed against each other as if they were mere seconds away from hot, sweaty sex.

"I can't," she said.

Yeah. He'd been expecting the red light. But then he considered that, maybe Gabrielle meant she couldn't because it'd only been six weeks since she'd delivered Lucas. Great. He'd somehow managed to forget all about that.

"I'm sorry," Houston apologized. "Your body isn't ready for this."

Still staring at him, she shook her head. "No. I mean I can't because, well, because of you. Because of *us*," Gabrielle said. "Physically, I'm more than ready for you." Wincing, she shook her head. "And I have no idea why I just told you that."

Houston was glad she had. Partly anyway. It didn't make it any easier to move away from her, but it did give him hope that one day he'd have her in his bed. Or on this love seat. Location was unimportant.

He didn't want to think of the complication that would cause. Yeah. *What harm could it do?* was racing through his head and mocking him.

They sat there staring at each other, with their breathing too heavy and their gazes too locked. Both of them were obviously primed and ready, but Gabrielle was right. Physically, all the pieces were in place, but the timing was far from right.

She groaned, stood up and squeezed her eyes shut. "Why this? Why now?"

He shook his head and shrugged at the obvious answer he was about to give her. "You're an attractive woman, and I want you. It's as simple as that."

"It's never as simple as that."

Houston begged to differ, mainly because he didn't want to look beyond this as a simple attraction. Since she'd given birth to Lucas, that might be playing into it. But for now, the attraction was strong enough to justify this burning need. And he'd leave it at that.

His phone buzzed, indicating he had a call. After waking up Lucas the day before, Houston had changed the ring tone to something much softer. He glanced down at the caller ID and saw that it was a call he'd been waiting for.

"Sheriff Whitley," Houston said, greeting the caller.

Gabrielle was obviously interested in what the sheriff had to say, because she sat back down next to Houston. He switched the call to speaker.

"My deputy just found Harlan Cordell," the sheriff explained.

"Where?" Houston immediately wanted to know. The house was locked down, and the security system was on, but those things weren't foolproof. That's why Houston had slept with a gun next to his bed.

"Cordell was at a hotel over on Miller's Creek. We got him, Houston. He's in custody and on the way here to my office."

"I'm on my way there, too," Houston said, standing.

"Good. Because the first thing Cordell said was that he wanted to talk to you and Gabrielle Markham."

"Gabrielle?" he questioned. "Why?"

"Cordell says he's got some news about who's after her, and he wants to tell Gabrielle that news to her face."

GABRIELLE'S FIRST IMPRESSION of Harlan Cordell was that he was slimy. Her second impression, he was dangerous.

Her stomach knotted just looking at him, even though the sheriff and his deputy were standing between Cordell and her. There wasn't much of a chance that Cordell would come after her right there in the Willow Ridge sheriff's office, but Houston apparently thought that was a strong possibility.

He caught on to her arm and anchored her in the doorway of the lone interrogation room. That put her a good fifteen feet from Cordell, who was seated at a gray metal table, but she had no trouble seeing every detail of his expression.

Cordell smiled at her.

It was creepy, and it went with the rest of his appearance and demeanor. He was in his early forties, bulky at the shoulders and had signs of a double chin. His five-o'clock shadow was scruffy and well past the fashionable stage. So was he. His white shirt was wrinkled, and he looked as if he'd combed his copper-brown hair with his hand.

But then, according to the deputy, Cordell had spent most of the day before, and part of the night, trying to get to Houston and her.

Why? was the question Gabrielle wanted to ask him. But she wasn't certain she would get a straight answer from him.

"I wish you hadn't come," Houston whispered to her.

It wasn't his first objection. Gabrielle had lost count of exactly how many there had been on the twenty-five-minute drive from the ranch to the sheriff's office. But his protests had started almost immediately after Houston ended the call with the sheriff, and they had continued while she nursed Lucas so the baby wouldn't be hungry while she went into town to confront Cordell.

Houston had wanted to attend this meeting without her. He'd wanted to get the answers himself from Cordell. But this was her fight, and even though Gabrielle was exhausted and frightened for her baby's safety, she wouldn't let a goon like Harlan Cordell run all over her. She had to stop whatever he was planning to do to her. And maybe, if there was some evidence, she could do that by having him arrested.

Then she could figure out what to do about Houston.

In addition to everything else going on in her life, she had to get better control of her involvement with him, and that didn't include any more kissing sessions. That didn't mean she didn't *want* to kiss him... No, she wanted that, and more, from him.

It just meant it was best to keep this attraction at bay until they put an end to the danger and dealt with the issue of Lucas's custody.

"The sheriff's got no proof of my doing anything wrong," Cordell said. "I'm here out of the goodness of my heart, to do my civic duty."

Gabrielle looked at the sheriff. "Are there charges against him?"

"Not yet. They're still trying, but SAPD hasn't been

able to link him to the gunmen who held the women hostage."

"And they won't be able to do that," Cordell said. "I've done nothing wrong. Yes, those gunmen owed me money, but I wouldn't have committed murder and other various felonies for the sake of cash."

"You sure about that?" Houston asked in challenge. "Then why are you here if you're not up to something bad?"

"I was just visiting Willow Ridge and looking for you. No crime in doing that. For the record," Cordell added, staring right at her, "I was trying to do you a favor."

"How? By trying to run Houston and me off the road yesterday?" she fired back. Despite the shaky nerves, Gabrielle met his gaze head-on.

He shrugged. "That wasn't me."

Houston inched slightly forward. "We have a photo of you, stepping from the vehicle, that says otherwise."

"You're mistaken. It must have been someone who looks like me."

She glanced at the sheriff again for some kind of confirmation or denial. "The car he was driving wasn't black. And it didn't have any damage consistent with running someone off the road."

Gabrielle choked back a groan.

"What about his partner?" Houston demanded. "There were two men who got out at Jay Markham's apartment. That second man could have been the one driving the black car."

The sheriff shook his head. "When we picked up Cordell, he was alone."

That sent Houston's gaze slashing toward Cordell. "So, who's your partner?"

"Don't have one. I occasionally hire assistants, but most of time they just end up getting in the way. I prefer to do things myself."

"Like trying to hurt Gabrielle," Houston fired back.

"I wouldn't want to hurt her." Cordell's voice was calm and filled with mock concern. "But it doesn't surprise me something like that would have happened. You got any idea how much trouble your brother is in?"

Gabrielle folded her arms over her chest. "No. But I suppose you'll tell me."

"Gladly." He flashed another smile. "He owes me money. Lots of it. But I'm not the only one. Jay made some bad investments out at the horse racing park, and I figure someone wants to collect that money from you. With you being an attorney and all, I'm guessing you got some savings stashed away somewhere."

Gabrielle didn't intend to discuss her finances with this man.

"Is that what you were trying to do—collect Jay's debts from Gabrielle?" Houston demanded.

Cordell shook his head and dropped the smile when he looked at Houston. "I said it wasn't me who went after you, but Jay owes people who'd do something like that."

The sheriff moved a tablet of paper and a pen closer to Cordell. "I want the names of those people."

Another shrug from Cordell. "Don't know their names. You'd have to ask Jay about that."

Gabrielle huffed. This was another runaround, and after dealing with her brother the night before, she was tired of not having answers. "You said you knew who was after me," she reminded him.

The man looked ready to shrug again, but Houston pushed himself away from the door, moved in and bracketed his hands on the table. He was close enough to Cordell to violate his personal space. "Cut the BS. If you're not the one after Gabrielle, then who is? I also want to know how you knew she was here in Willow Ridge."

"I don't have a name," Cordell insisted. "And as for how I knew she was here, well, someone told me. In confidence."

Houston eased back and looked at the sheriff. "Arrest him. I have the photo of Cordell getting out of the black car that came after Gabrielle and me. That should be enough to take him into custody for attempted murder."

That surprised Gabrielle, but not as much as it surprised Cordell, when Houston started to walk away.

Cordell jumped to his feet. "Wait a minute. Doesn't 'in confidence' mean anything to you?" Cordell shook his head, and any trace of his smile vanished. "I don't want to make the wrong enemies."

"You already have," Houston assured him. "Because I'm your enemy now." And his low, dangerous tone left no room for any doubt about that.

Cordell and Houston had a staring match, and Gabrielle could see the exact moment when Cordell conceded that he was going to have to give them some real information. Houston was a formidable foe, and Cordell didn't want any part of that.

"Like I said, Jay owes me money, and when he told

me he couldn't pay, I started watching his place. I wanted to keep tabs on him and make sure he was doing everything possible to get me the cash. That's when I saw his visitors, and I figured out where Gabrielle was."

Houston glanced back at her, probably to see if she understood that comment, but she only shook her head.

"What visitors?" Houston demanded.

This time, when Cordell lifted his shoulder, the shrug seemed more genuine than cocky. "Your father, of course. Mack Sadler. I figured, if a man like Mack came out to see a man like Jay, then it probably had something to do with Gabrielle, so I took a drive out here to Willow Ridge—"

"My father came to see Jay?" Houston interrupted.

Cordell nodded, as if the answer were obvious.

Gabrielle tried not to react, but it was hard to remain calm after hearing that. Maybe Mack had gone to see her brother so he could, in turn, find Lucas and her, but if that's all there was to it, then why hadn't Mack volunteered that information?

"Cordell could be lying," Houston reminded her.

Gabrielle hung on to that as if it were a lifeline, because she truly didn't want Houston's father to have been the one who tried to hurt them. But just in case he was, Gabrielle didn't want Lucas at the ranch.

Mack could come back anytime.

"I have to get back to the ranch," Gabrielle insisted. She turned, but then stopped when Cordell called out to her.

"I'm not the one after you," Cordell insisted, when she glanced back at him. "You got a lot more trouble on your hands than just me if you're trusting the Sadlers."

Gabrielle slowly turned back around to face him. "What does that mean?"

"It means, Mack wasn't alone when he visited your brother day before yesterday. There was another man with him."

She pulled back her shoulders. "You're not suggesting Houston was there."

"No. Not Houston. But the next best thing. His foreman, Dale Burnett."

Chapter Nine

"Hurry," Gabrielle insisted.

Houston did. He caught on to her hand, and together they raced out of the sheriff's office. They jumped into his silver Porsche and sped out of the parking lot.

This would no doubt be the longest twenty-five-minute drive of their lives.

Gabrielle took out her phone from her purse. Houston didn't have to ask who she was calling. He knew. She needed to get in touch with Lily Rose.

"I don't want to scare you," Gabrielle said, when the nanny answered, "but I need you to keep Lucas with you at all times, and lock your door." She paused. "I'll explain everything as soon as I get there. Just don't leave your room."

After slapping the phone shut, she yelled "Hurry" to Houston.

"Remember, Cordell could be lying," Houston reminded her.

"I know, but I can't take that chance."

Neither could he. Houston trusted Dale, or at least he thought he could. After all, he'd known Dale for the better part of twenty years; but Houston also knew his father, and Mack could be a persuasive man. It was possible that Mack had talked Dale into doing something stupid.

Like visiting Jay.

Still, even if Cordell had told the truth about that, it didn't mean his foreman would have done anything to hurt Gabrielle, Lucas or him. But if that were so, Dale should have been the one to tell him about the visit to Jay. He shouldn't have had to learn something that big from Harlan Cordell.

The anger slammed through Houston. He was damn tired of all the lies and lies by omission. One way or another, he would get to the bottom of this, even if it meant grilling his father and Dale.

Houston pressed harder on the accelerator, once he was beyond the town limits and away from other vehicles. Beside him, Gabrielle had a death grip on her cell phone, probably so she could answer it immediately, if Lily Rose called back to tell her of some problem that had arisen at the ranch.

"It'll be okay," Houston tried to assure her, but he knew there was no way he could guarantee that.

He considered calling someone else at the ranch, maybe one of the maids or another ranch hand, but he didn't have their personal numbers. If he dialed any of the landlines at the house, Dale would be the one to answer, since all calls were routed through his desk phone or cell. Houston didn't want the man to have any kind of heads-up or warning when he confronted him about what Cordell had said.

But there was one person he could call.

Houston took out his cell, scrolled through the

numbers and made the call to his father. The phone rang and rang, and then went to voicemail.

That didn't soothe Houston's temper.

"I need to speak to you now," Houston said, leaving the message for his father.

He hung up and was about to try yet again to comfort Gabrielle, but then he saw a white car in his rearview mirror.

Even though this was a country road that led primarily to the ranch, it wasn't unusual for there to be other traffic. Still, Houston got an uneasy feeling, and that uneasy feeling went up a notch because he couldn't see the driver or anyone else in the vehicle. The dark-tinted windows prevented that. So did the sun bouncing off the glass.

"What?" she asked.

Gabrielle had obviously noticed his expression, and she followed his gaze to the rearview mirror. Then she looked behind them.

"You don't think..." But she didn't finish the thought.

Houston didn't want to finish it, either. He focused on the road ahead, specifically the curves and the rickety wooden bridge that he practically flew across. He damn sure didn't want to wreck the Porsche just because of an eerie gut feeling about the car behind them.

The car that was going way too fast.

Houston checked the speedometer and saw he was pushing seventy. The other car was going faster than that, because it was quickly eating up the distance between them.

In a straight-line race, the Porsche wouldn't have any

trouble outrunning the other car, but there was nothing straight about this road. In addition to the curves and three different creeks, there were deep ditches, slick clay banks and massive trees that grew just a few feet from the asphalt surface. Under ideal situations, it was like driving an obstacle course.

This wasn't an ideal situation.

His heart was pounding, his mind racing. And the only thing he wanted to do was hurry back to the ranch and make sure Lucas was safe.

He had to slow down to take one of the curves, but Houston was still going so fast that the tires squealed. The Porsche fishtailed coming out of the turn, but he straightened it out and jammed the accelerator again.

The white car did the same.

"Should I call someone?" Gabrielle asked.

Houston considered it, but he was literally halfway between town and the ranch. Another fifteen minutes tops, and he would reach his property. After that, he could make sure Gabrielle was safe so he could confront whoever the hell was in that car.

"Don't call anyone just yet. It could be teenagers out for a joy ride," he reminded Gabrielle and himself.

He had to slow down to take another curve. This one came out at the second of three bridges they would have to cross. Houston made it through those obstacles and onto a mile stretch of straight road. Here's where he could make up some time and get farther ahead of the car behind them.

Or so he thought.

Houston glanced in the rearview mirror and saw the

hand snake out from the driver's side window. But it wasn't just a hand.

The hand held a gun.

"Get down!" Houston shouted to Gabrielle.

She looked behind them, no doubt to see why he'd shouted that warning, but Houston didn't want her to waste a second responding. He caught on to her shoulder and shoved her deeper into the seat.

He heard the blast.

Even though his windows were up and the Porsche engine was humming, he had no trouble hearing the shot that the SOB had fired at them.

It must have missed, because the glass didn't break, and there was no sound to indicate the bullet had torn through the car.

But the guy fired again. And again.

The third shot went through the Porsche's back windshield and shattered the safety glass. Worse, the web of cracked glass made it impossible for Houston to see through the rearview mirror. He checked the one on the side.

Just as another shot slammed into his car.

"Get the gun from the glove compartment," he told Gabrielle. Not that he could return fire. And he sure didn't want her trying to do that, either. But he wanted the gun ready just in case. "And go ahead and call nine one one so we can get the sheriff out here."

Houston kept his attention nailed to the road ahead, while Gabrielle made the call and then fished through the glove compartment to come up with his Smith and Wesson.

"Hold on to it," he said, hoping like hell that they wouldn't need it.

He continued to speed ahead.

And the bullets continued to come at them. Being on the straight stretch of the road suddenly didn't have as many advantages at it had before. The Porsche was in the direct line of fire.

"Who's doing this?" she asked, trying to look into the side mirror.

Houston shoved her right back down. "I don't know." Maybe it was someone working for Cordell. After all, there'd been two men in the black car that had tried to run Gabrielle and him off the road. Of course, it could be someone else.

He pushed any theories aside. He didn't have time to speculate now. Later though, he would get answers.

Houston felt the steering wheel jerk to the right. Not a gentle tug, either. It suddenly seemed locked in place, and he knew why.

The gunman had managed to shoot out the tire.

Hell.

He began to pump the brakes, but he no longer had control of the car.

"Hold on," Houston warned Gabrielle.

He couldn't keep them on the road. The Porsche was headed straight for the water-filled ditch that dropped down at least four feet from the surface of the road.

From the corner of his eye, he made sure Gabrielle was wearing her seat belt. She was. But he knew that wouldn't necessarily be enough protection when they crashed. And there was no *if* in this equation. They *would* crash.

Houston only hoped he could minimize the impact so that Gabrielle wouldn't be hurt. He thought of Lucas, of how important it was for Gabrielle and him to get out of this situation, but there were no guarantees that would happen.

"Don't drop the gun," he told her. Because he was dead certain he would need it to protect Gabrielle. That gunman would come after them once the Porsche had been stopped.

Houston grappled with the steering wheel, though his efforts were useless. The Porsche's front tires left the asphalt, plowing them through the soft ground. The car did a nosedive right into the ditch.

The airbags instantly deployed and slammed against Gabrielle and him. Houston didn't take the time to figure out if he was injured or not. He batted aside their airbags and grabbed the gun from her.

"Stay down," he warned her, and Houston reached to open his door. But it was jammed.

Cursing, he rammed his shoulder against it and tried to use what was left of his side mirror to get a visual on the white car. He couldn't see it, but that didn't mean it wasn't there. The gunman had succeeded in getting them to crash, and now he was probably coming in for the kill.

"The car's filling up with water," Gabrielle let him know.

Yes. He could feel it swirling around his feet, but hopefully the ditch wasn't deep enough for the water to be as much of a threat as the guy who'd put a bullet in his tire. He needed for Gabrielle to be able to stay in the Porsche and use it for cover.

Houston gave the door another shove, and this time it gave way. He practically spilled out into the ditch, but he kept his gun raised so it wouldn't get wet, and so he'd be ready to return fire.

He glanced around, but he soon had a clear idea of where the gunman was—when the man fired another shot.

The bullet went through the door, only inches from where Houston was crouched. The guy was already too close, and the sheriff probably wouldn't arrive for another ten minutes or more. Gabrielle could be dead by then.

But Houston didn't intend to let that happen.

He used the Porsche for cover and looked over the top until he spotted the white car. It was there, stopped on the road, and from what he could tell, the driver was still inside, with only his hand sticking out from the window.

Houston took aim at the front windshield and fired.

The shot burst through the glass. But he didn't stop there. He fired again. And again.

The driver jerked back his hand, and Houston heard him throw the car into gear. For one horrifying moment, Houston thought the guy might try to ram into them, and if so, Gabrielle would be a sitting duck.

Houston started to yell for her to get out, even though it was a huge risk. She could be shot before she managed to get behind one of the trees. The closest one at this point was still a good fifteen feet away.

But the driver didn't come after them.

He gunned the engine.

He was getting away.

That couldn't happen. Gabrielle and he couldn't continue to go through these attacks, because next time they might not be so lucky.

Houston pivoted, the cold mud and water sloshing over his legs, and he took aim at the car. He fired. He didn't hit the tire, but the bullet slammed into the back bumper.

Cursing, Houston barreled out of the ditch and climbed out of the sharp incline so he could get back onto the road. He took aim again and fired into the white car.

The driver didn't stop.

Neither did Houston. With his gun still ready and aimed, he went running after the SOB who'd just tried to kill them.

Chapter Ten

"I should have gotten him," Gabrielle heard Houston say to Sheriff Whitley. He added some profanity to that. "I should have at least managed to get the license plate."

She disagreed with him. She wanted to tell Houston that it would have been next to impossible for him to chase down that car while he was on foot. She also wanted to remind him that the car's license plates had been obscured with mud or something. But her teeth were chattering, and she couldn't manage to say anything as she sat in the back of the police cruiser.

Houston and she had come close to being killed today.

For weeks the danger, or at least the possibility of danger, had been much too close for comfort, but today she'd come face-to-face with it, when the gunman had fired God knows how many shots into Houston's Porsche. Any one of those shots could have hit them, and they were lucky to have escaped with just a few nicks and muddy clothes.

"My deputy will find the person who did this to you," the sheriff insisted.

She didn't doubt the deputy would try, but the reality

was the man had a huge head start. The gunman had sped away a good five minutes before the sheriff and his deputy arrived. Those five minutes gave the person plenty of time to disappear.

Of course, he could—and probably would—come back. Gabrielle didn't think this was over.

Houston was sitting beside her in the backseat, his hand pressed over hers, their fingers linked. He hadn't let go of her since the sheriff had ushered them into the cruiser. Gabrielle was thankful for that. She didn't consider herself a weak woman, but she was afraid that Houston's touch was the only thing that was holding her together.

Even though they were just a few minutes from the ranch, Houston called again and spoke to Greta, the maid. He asked about Lucas, and about his father and Dale. Judging from Houston's reaction, he didn't care much for whatever the maid said. He closed the phone so hard she was surprised it didn't break.

"What's wrong?" Gabrielle held her breath and started to pray. Lucas had to be all right.

"The baby's fine," Houston immediately assured her.

Gabrielle nearly went limp with relief. "Then what made you so upset?" Because everything would be minor, compared to her son's safety.

"Dale's not at the ranch. He drove into San Antonio on business."

Oh...she understood his reaction then. That could be true—Dale might have left for a valid reason. But if they were to believe Harlan Cordell, then Dale might be in on whatever was happening to Houston and her.

What was happening? Gabrielle asked herself.

Was this connected to the maternity hostages, or did this all have to do with Lucas?

"You asked about your father?" she questioned.

Houston nodded. "I just want to make sure he hadn't returned the ranch. He didn't."

That was something, at least. They already had enough to worry about, without Mack's return. Of course, they would eventually have to deal with Houston's father, and even Dale. Right now though, she only wanted to get to her son.

The moment the sheriff came to a stop in front of the ranch house, Gabrielle barreled out of the car. Houston did the same, and they practically ran to the porch and up the steps. Lily Rose must have been watching from the window, because she met them at the top of the stairs.

"Lucas is fine," she whispered. "He's still sleeping." While her voice was calm, her eyes and expression conveyed her alarm and concern. It probably didn't help that Houston and she looked as if they'd literally just climbed out of a giant mud hole.

On the drive to the ranch, Houston had filled the nanny in on what had happened to them, but he'd kept the details sketchy. However, Gabrielle figured Lily Rose could fill in the blanks. The woman knew there was trouble brewing.

"I need to be with Lucas," Gabrielle told Lily Rose. "We both need that," she added, after glancing at Houston's face.

Gabrielle kept her steps soft, but she hurried past the nanny and into her room. She made a beeline for the crib, and just as Lily Rose had said, Lucas was still sleeping, and in the exact position she'd left him a little over an hour and a half ago, when she'd fed him so that Houston and she could go into town and confront Cordell.

Houston came in behind her, shutting the door and locking it. That engaged lock was a stark reminder that they still might not be safe, even though they were inside and away from that gunman.

He stood next to her while they both looked down at the baby. They didn't have to voice their relief, because she knew he was feeling the same thing she was. She had to fight the urge to pick Lucas up, but that would only wake him. If he stayed in his routine, he would nap for at least another half hour, maybe more. There was no reason to disrupt his sleep, simply because she was falling apart.

"You need to get out of those wet clothes," Houston told her.

Gabrielle glanced at her clothes and knew he was right. Still…

"I won't leave him," Houston promised her. "I'll stay right here, next to him."

She nodded and realized just how much that promise meant to her. At this moment, there was only one person she would trust as much as herself to protect and defend Lucas, and it was Houston.

How ironic.

The man who could cost her the most, her son, was the only man she wanted near her right now.

Gabrielle grabbed a pair of clean jeans and a white top from her suitcase and hurried to the bathroom. She hadn't brought a lot of clothes with her to the ranch, only the items she'd had with her at the motel, and she was quickly running out of things to wear. She had plenty of outfits at her house in San Antonio, but she couldn't go back there.

So where should she go?

She couldn't stay at the ranch forever, even though Houston would no doubt put up a fight if Gabrielle announced she was leaving anytime soon. Still, she had to do something. She couldn't just continue to react to the dangerous situations going on around them. She needed a plan.

Gabrielle made a mental note to arrange for a bodyguard. Even if that bodyguard had to do temporary duty at the ranch with Lucas and her, at least that was a start to regaining some of the independence she'd surrendered when she walked onto the ranch the day before.

She quickly changed and went back into the bedroom. True to his word, Houston was still keeping watch over Lucas, but he also had his phone pressed to his ear. His voice was practically a whisper, so she couldn't hear his conversation, but she prayed nothing else had gone wrong.

Houston had also removed his stained shirt, probably because he'd anticipated changing, once she was back in the room. He had it slung over his shoulder. He likely hadn't meant for his bare torso to grab her attention, but it did.

"Dale's on his way back," Houston relayed to her, when he ended the call.

Her heart was still racing, and that didn't help. "You said you could trust him. Do you still believe that?"

He nodded. "But that doesn't mean I won't ask him

some tough questions. If he helped my father, I don't think he'll lie about it."

No. But he might not tell the truth about the extent of his "help." Still, she wanted the chance to confront Dale, just in case he did know the person who'd fired those shots at Houston and her.

She glanced down at Houston's jeans and boots. The mud went all the way up to his knees. "Your turn," she said. "Go ahead and change."

He turned as if he might do that, but then he stopped and stared at her. He reached out and moved a strand of hair off her cheek. "I would ask if you're okay, but I can tell you aren't. You're shaking."

Gabrielle didn't even attempt to deny it, or try to make him believe it was from the cold, wet clothes that she'd just shed. "I guess I'm not used to people trying to kill me."

She'd meant it as a stupid joke, something to help lighten the mood. But she failed miserably. Much to her disgust, Gabrielle felt the tears well up in her eyes, and her throat snapped shut.

No!

She didn't want to cry in front of Houston. For that matter, she didn't want to cry at all. She was so tired of feeling helpless.

On a heavy sigh, Houston tossed his shirt onto the nearby chair, slipped his arm around her and pulled her to him. "For the record, I think you did damn good when we were under fire."

She looked up at him to thank him, but the words were suddenly lost. Everything seemed to stop and pinpoint right on Houston. He'd saved her life today. He had gotten her safely back to Lucas. And he'd endangered himself doing that.

"What?" he asked.

Gabrielle shook her head, hoping to clear it, but everything stayed fuzzy. Everything in her mind, that is. Her body seemed to know exactly what it wanted to do.

She came up on her toes and put her mouth to his.

He made a slight sound of surprise that rumbled deep in his throat, but the surprise obviously didn't last. Houston snapped her to him and kissed her right back.

Yes!

That was the one word that made it through the fuzziness in her brain. Yes, this was what she needed. Yes, the kiss would get her through this. It was stupid logic of course. On some level she understood that, but she also understood that she wasn't going to stop.

Neither did Houston.

The kiss continued, and it didn't remain merely a gesture of reassurance. It quickly turned hot, and Houston used his tongue to go past her lips and into her mouth.

His taste was instant. All male, all need. It was yet something else to kindle the heat that was already starting to demand that this kiss go deeper and further.

Houston took things further without her having to ask him.

His arms wound tighter around her, and he turned, moving her against the wall. Gabrielle took things further, as well. She caught on to the back of Houston's neck and pulled him down toward her. Not that their mouths could get any closer, but Gabrielle got a cheap thrill out of the small amount of control when their bodies pressed each other.

Houston responded with another of his throaty sounds. This one wasn't of surprise but rather of pure pleasure.

Something she totally understood.

Kissing Houston sent a spear of pleasure right through her.

But soon, very soon, kissing didn't seem to be enough. They grappled for position, and Gabrielle squeezed her hand between them so she could touch his chest. Houston went after her neck and landed some of those hot kisses there.

The fire inside her spiked.

Gabrielle reminded herself that Lucas wasn't far away. But he was asleep. And he was too young to realize that she was carrying on with his biological father. Still, she decided to put a little space between the crib and them, and she maneuvered Houston toward the sitting area of her suite.

The neck kisses didn't stop.

Neither did the caresses she managed on his chest. He was toned and lean, all man, and his body wasn't the product of a gym, but no doubt hours of working on the ranch.

She was trying to make it to the love seat, but they stopped near the door. All in all, a good idea. Gabrielle was on fire now, and without having to move, she could concentrate on what to do about that fire.

Houston obviously had some ideas.

He cupped her bottom, lifting her just enough so that his sex met hers. He was huge, hard and ready. And Gabrielle was suddenly ready, as well. All she could think about was having sex with him and finding some relief for the pressure cooker of heat that was roaring inside her.

She wanted to pull him to the floor and have him take her there. She wanted him inside her *now,* and she didn't want to think of logic and consequences.

But she *had* to think of those things.

Gabrielle pulled back and caught on to his shoulder, forcing eye contact. His breath was gusting, as was hers, and she could see the pulse hammer in his throat.

"Bad timing," he mumbled.

That was a massive understatement, but the truth was, there'd been no good time for kissing Houston. Not since she'd come to the ranch, anyway. And she doubted the timing would be good anytime soon. Still, she didn't regret what had just happened.

Which made her feel stupid. She'd never been one to fall head over heels, but that's what was happening to her now.

"It's been a long time since I've felt that," he added.

Oh. So, he had the late-wife baggage in addition to the old bad blood between them. Neither felt like obstacles right now, but with her body still burning and begging, everything seemed manageable, and it was that kind of attitude that would get her in even more trouble. She was about to remind Houston and herself of that, but his phone buzzed.

Maybe because he'd anticipated the conversation they'd been about to have, he seemed relieved to get the call. At least he did until he glanced at the caller ID and frowned.

"Dale," Houston said, answering the call.

She understood the frown, but she also understood

why he quickly took Dale's call. After the allegations Cordell had made, Houston no doubt had some questions to put to his foreman. But Gabrielle was hoping that Dale could clear his name. They already had enough people to worry about, without adding Dale to that list.

"You what?" Houston demanded.

And her heart dropped. His tone and expression told her that something was indeed wrong.

"You thought that was a good idea?" Houston asked the caller, and he had sarcasm dripping from his voice.

Another pause. Gabrielle tried to hear what was making Houston angrier by the moment, but she could only hear the murmur of Dale's voice.

"I'll be right down," Houston snarled. He closed the phone and looked at her. "Dale's back, and he's not alone. Apparently, both my father and Salvador Franks are here too."

Oh, mercy. She didn't have the energy to deal with Dale, much less the trio. "What do they want?"

"To *talk*," he said, as if it were profanity. He glanced down at his pants and then at her. "I don't suppose you'd be willing to wait here while I meet with them?"

It was tempting, especially since the fatigue was starting to set in, but if one of the men was the person who'd just attacked them on the road, Gabrielle didn't want to hide away in her room while Houston dealt with it alone.

He must have realized what her answer was, because he tipped his head toward Lily Rose's room. "Have her stay with Lucas. And I want the door locked. Just give me a minute to change."

She nodded, and while Houston went next door to

his room, she knocked on the nanny's door. Lily Rose answered right away, so Gabrielle had her go into the room with Lucas. And she didn't leave until she heard Lily Rose engage the locks.

Gabrielle hoped that was just a precaution, and that the danger wouldn't make its way up the stairs to her son.

She went to Houston's room, and since the door was already open, she looked inside.

And got an eyeful.

He was butt naked, and in the process of stepping into his boxers.

"Sorry," she mumbled, and she started to close her eyes. But for some reason, her eyes didn't cooperate.

Houston's face wasn't the only thing hot about him. So was his body. She'd been right about the toned part, and that applied not to just his chest but his abs and butt, as well. And Gabrielle felt like an idiot for noticing that at a time like this.

"Trust me," Houston mumbled back, "if I had a choice, both of us would be getting naked right now."

She felt her face flush. The rest of her went hot, too, and she wondered just how strong this attraction was, that it would override the dread she should be feeling about the meeting with Dale, Mack and Salvador?

Gabrielle hoped it was simply an attraction and nothing more, but she was afraid she'd crossed yet another line with Houston. And that made her a double idiot. Because, if she fell hard for him, then a broken heart was in her near future. There was no way a man like him would fall for a woman like her.

Houston pulled on a clean pair of jeans and a blue

shirt that was almost identical in color to his eyes. His boots went on next, and then he reached for the gun he had on his dresser.

That got her attention in a different kind of way. The heat vanished, and her concerns returned full force.

"You think that's necessary?" she asked.

Houston shrugged and tucked the gun in the back waist of his jeans. "I don't know anymore what's necessary and what isn't." He headed for the door but stopped.

And he kissed her.

It wasn't a quick peck of reassurance. It was a full kiss to remind her that they had some personal things to work out, and that working them out would almost certainly land them in bed.

Houston let her go, gave her a look of regret that they couldn't immediately finish what they'd started and then headed for the stairs. Gabrielle was right behind him, and it didn't take her long to see their visitors. All three of them were in the sitting room just off the foyer. Salvador was seated, Dale was standing next to him and Mack was at the bar, fixing himself a drink.

"Hell of a mess you're in," Mack announced to Houston right away, and he finished off the shot he'd just poured. "Are you all right, son?"

"Yeah," Houston answered, but not before a long pause and a glance at all of them. "Did the three of you come together?"

Mack shook his head. "I asked Salvador to meet me here."

Gabrielle didn't wait for Mack to ask about her well-being. She aimed her attention at Dale. "Before someone tried to kill us, we'd just spoken with Harlan Cordell. He said both Mack and you went to my brother's apartment."

Dale tipped his eyes to the ceiling and cursed. What he didn't do was deny it.

"I took Dale with me," Mack volunteered. "With Jay's hot head and all, I didn't know if I'd need backup when I went to ask him your whereabouts."

"I swear, Houston, that's the only reason we went," Dale explained. "I didn't know about anything that had happened at Cryogen. Mack just said he might need some muscle. Hell, I didn't even know where we were going until we got there."

Houston took a step closer to Dale and met him eye to eye. "And you didn't think it was important to tell me that my father had taken you to see Gabrielle's brother?"

"I didn't know this had anything to do with Gabrielle," Dale insisted.

"He didn't," Mack confirmed. "I told him I needed to see Jay about the lawsuit, that I'd heard rumors he was filing another one."

Gabrielle looked at both Mack and Dale, and even though it might be naïve of her, she believed them. Or maybe she just wanted to believe that Dale hadn't betrayed Houston.

His father was a different matter.

Mack might be telling the truth about Dale accompanying him for that visit, but she wasn't sure that he had come clean about everything else.

She folded her arms over her chest. "Here's what I think," Gabrielle started, and she stared at Mack. "I suspect that, when you learned that Lizzy's embryo was at the Cryogen Clinic, that you and Salvador here worked out a deal. You used me for a surrogate."

Salvador jumped to his feet. "No!" And he was adamant about it, too. "It's a clerical error, just as I said." But then he dodged her gaze.

Houston switched his attention from Dale to Salvador. "If you have something to add, you'd better do it now."

Gabrielle took note of everyone's expressions, and for the first time since she'd met him, Mack seemed concerned. Dale just appeared riled, and embarrassed that he'd been brought into all of this.

Of course, Dale could be faking his outrage.

She still wasn't ready to trust anyone but Houston.

"Your father pressured me," Salvador finally said. "He didn't want you to know that Ms. Markham was carrying your child."

"You SOB," Mack howled, smacking the glass down onto the bar.

Houston ignored Mack's string of name calling and kept his attention fastened on Salvador. "Did my father say why he wanted to keep that secret?"

Salvador looked away again. "Because once the child was born, he wanted me to, uh, coerce Ms. Markham into giving you the baby."

That sent Mack storming across the room, and he would have grabbed Salvador by the jacket if Dale hadn't stepped in his path.

Dale aimed his index finger at Mack. "You stay put," he warned.

Salvador swallowed hard before he continued. "After the baby was born, I was supposed to go to Ms. Markham and tell her about the mix-up. I was also supposed to show her doctored papers that would have indicated that her brother knew what was going on."

"What?" Gabrielle said, with a gasp.

Houston's "what?" was said through clenched teeth.

"I was to convince her that, if she didn't give up the child, then her brother would be arrested. She probably would be arrested, too. Then I was to offer her a seven-figure compensation, along with covering all her expenses and offering her a new embryo."

In disbelief, she lifted her hands, palms up, and shook her head. "And you thought this plan would work?"

Salvador drew in a deep breath. "I believe Mack Sadler was counting on the high probability that you would protect your brother, and yourself."

Gabrielle found that laughable and outrageous. She stared at Mack to see if he would deny any of what Salvador had just said. He didn't. He just looked defiantly at her.

"I was obviously wrong about you," Mack mumbled. "But everything I did, I had Houston in mind. My son was hurting, and he needed something to heal him."

"I was doing just fine, Dad," Houston mumbled back. He turned to Dale. "I'm disappointed that you had any part in this."

Dale nodded. "I'll gather my things and leave."

Houston caught on to his arm. "For now, why don't you just take some time off? A paid vacation. It'll give us both a chance to figure out where this needs to go."

"And what about me?" Mack's voice boomed through the room. "You plan to send me away again, too?" But his arrogant tone indicated he didn't believe Houston would do that.

Houston walked closer to his father. "Yes."

The arrogance vanished from Mack's eyes. "For how long?"

"I don't know. I'll leave that up to Gabrielle. When and if she ever forgives you, then I'll think about doing the same."

"You can't mean that," Mack insisted.

"But I do." And Houston left no doubt about that.

Mack went closer to him. "The ends justify the means. You have a son, and judging from the fact that you've got Gabrielle here under your roof, and probably in your bed, you're damn close to having that family you always wanted."

Houston went toward his father, but Gabrielle latched on to him to hold him back. She'd had enough violence for one day.

"How can you fault me for trying to give you that baby?" Mack asked. "I didn't put all of this into motion. The clinic screwed up. I just wanted to fix that screwup by giving you what's rightfully yours."

Houston's eyes stayed narrowed, and she could practically feel the tension tightening his body. "Oh, I can fault you, all right, because you were dead wrong to try to manipulate Gabrielle." Houston looked at Dale. "We'll talk after a day or two."

Dale nodded, apologized again, and headed for the door. Salvador excused himself, as well, and left.

Mack stayed.

"We're blood," Mack reminded him, and then he looked past Houston and at her. "Tell me, do you regret you got Lucas?"

"No." And Gabrielle meant that. Even if she could,

she wouldn't go back and undo things and get a different embryo. "But I don't trust you. And right now I prefer to be in the company of people I can trust."

"Leave now," Houston ordered his father.

Mack glared at both of them, and for a moment she thought there might be a fight after all, but then Mack stormed toward the door. He slammed it shut behind him.

Houston stood there, staring down at the floor, and then he went to the front door to lock it. He also reset the security system.

"I'm sorry," Gabrielle told him.

"Don't be. My father is the one who should be apologizing." He turned back around to face her. "For the record, I don't want you in my bed because you gave birth to Lucas. I don't want you there because it'll score some kind of brownie points if we have custody issues. I want you there because I want you. And that's all there is to it."

Gabrielle didn't have any real doubts about that, because she understood the attraction between them. That attraction didn't have anything to do with Lucas. She was sure of that now. Of course, in some ways that only made things more complicated.

Houston reached out, slid his hand around the back of her neck and eased her to him. "I'm not like my father," he promised her.

"I never thought you were." And because she needed to reassure him and herself, Gabrielle kissed him.

She probably would have kept on kissing him, too, but there was a knock at the door.

Houston cursed. "That better not be my dad." He glanced out the window next to the door and froze.

"What?" Gabrielle asked. She didn't wait for Houston to explain that look of shock and concern on his face, she moved to the side so she could see for herself.

And what Gabrielle saw was the blood.

Chapter Eleven

Hell. "What now?" Houston mumbled.

Gabrielle tried to push her way past him, but he stopped her and looked around the front yard. Even though his first instinct was to rush out onto the porch, as well, Houston knew that wasn't a smart thing to do after everything that had already happened today.

He took out his cell and passed it to Gabrielle. "Call nine one one," he instructed.

The color had drained from her face, and she was staring at her brother who was leaning against one of the pristine, white porch columns. Jay was clutching his left arm.

"I've been shot," Jay managed to say.

Houston had already figured out that part. There was blood on his green shirt sleeve, and some of that blood had splattered onto the porch.

"Stay inside," Houston warned Gabrielle, doubting that she would, but at least the nine-one-one call would keep her occupied for several seconds.

"I've been shot," Jay repeated. With the column supporting his back, he slid to a sitting position.

Despite the risk, Houston couldn't just let him die. Jay

might be a scumbag, but he was Gabrielle's brother. So he hurried out to the man, but he also kept watch of their surroundings, in case this was some kind of ambush. His father, Salvador Franks and Dale had already driven away, so the front lawn and drive were empty, except for an older model red car. Jay's probably.

Did that mean Jay had driven from his apartment to the ranch after someone had shot him?

Or was this some kind of trick?

Behind him, Houston heard Gabrielle ask the emergency dispatcher for an ambulance. Her voice was frantic, and the moment she finished the call, she ran out onto the porch and knelt down next to her brother.

"Who did this to you?" she asked.

"I don't know." Jay shook his head and closed his eyes for a moment. "I was on my way out to see you, and when I slowed down to make that last turn to the ranch, someone shot me. The window was down, and the bullet went right into my arm."

Houston hadn't heard a shot, but that didn't mean there hadn't been one. After all, the discussion he'd had with his father had gotten pretty loud.

"Was the shooter driving a white car?" Houston asked.

Jay gave another head shake. "I didn't see who did this." He looked up at Houston. "I thought it might be you or your father."

Despite the gut punch of an accusation, Houston picked up the man and hauled him into the foyer. He kicked the door shut behind them. He hated the idea of bringing Jay into the house with Lucas just upstairs, but he preferred that Gabrielle be inside, in case there was another attack. There was no way Houston would get her to do that if her brother was still on the porch.

Greta, the maid, came running into the foyer. When she saw Jay and the blood, she gasped and pressed her hand to her mouth.

"Set the security system," Houston told the maid. "Arm the entire house and turn on all the surveillance cameras."

And he wished he could be giving these orders to Dale. Dale knew the security system better than anyone else on the ranch. Too bad Houston wasn't sure he could trust the man.

Greta first used the panel by the front door to arm it. That meant, if anyone opened a window or a door, the alarm would sound. Then she hurried toward Dale's office on the ground floor, where the main system was located.

Houston unclamped Jay's right hand from his injured arm, and he ripped open the shirt sleeve. There was a two-inch gash on his outer left arm, and it was bleeding.

"Just hang on," Gabrielle whispered to Jay. "The ambulance will be here soon."

Her brother nodded and dragged his tongue over his bottom lip. "I came out to warn you, sis." Jay stopped and drew in a ragged breath. "I had to tell you that he'll try to kill you again."

Gabrielle pulled back her shoulders. "*Who* will try to kill me?"

Jay took his time answering. "Mack Sadler."

Houston stared at Jay a moment before looking at Gabrielle. She didn't seem surprised, and that cut him to the core. Because, while he knew his father could be manipulative, Houston had never thought that manipulation would extend to physically hurting someone.

"Why do you think my father wants to kill Gabrielle?" Houston asked, pressing Jay.

"Because of Lucas." Jay moved his hand back over his arm and winced in pain.

Houston mentally winced, as well. He figured he knew where this was going.

"Your father called me two days ago. He wanted to know where Gabrielle was, and he offered me ten grand if I'd tell him." Jay shook his head. "But I didn't know where she was. Mack must have thought I was lying, because he upped the money. I told him I'd help. I had to," he added, giving his sister a pleading look.

"Why?" she asked.

"Because of the money I owe. I didn't want to help Mack. Honestly, I didn't. But I've got people who'll kill me if I don't come up with the cash."

"But you couldn't help my father," Houston pointed out, "because you didn't know where Gabrielle was."

Jay nodded frantically. "That's right. I didn't know. But Mack kept pressing. He thought if he pressed me hard enough, that I'd come up with your location."

"Mack wanted to find me so he'd find Lucas," Gabrielle mumbled. Was it Houston's imagination, or did she seem skeptical about what her brother was saying? "What does that have to do with him wanting me dead?"

Jay glanced at both of them, then winced again. "He didn't come out and say he intended to kill you, but that's the gist I got. He wants you out of the way so Houston can get full custody of Lucas."

Houston wanted to call the man a liar, but he couldn't. After the stunt his father had pulled at the Cryogen Clinic with Salvador Franks, Houston wasn't ready to trust Mack anytime soon.

But he wasn't about to trust Jay, either.

Houston glanced at the wound again and used Jay's shirt to wipe away the blood. He frowned. "That seems pretty superficial."

Jay's eyes widened. So did Gabrielle's. Houston braced himself for verbal fire from both of them for suggesting that Jay might have shot himself to gain his sister's sympathy.

And gain access to the ranch.

"Why would I do this to myself?" Jay asked, his voice sounding weaker. Or at least, he was making himself sound that way.

Houston shrugged. He was guessing this was about the money Jay owed. He stooped down and checked Jay for a weapon. He didn't find one, but that didn't mean he didn't have a gun stashed in his car.

He heard the hurried footsteps coming from the hall, and Houston looked over his shoulder to see Greta running their way. "Sir, I did as you asked, but you need to see the security monitor. When I turned on those cameras like you asked, I saw someone. It looks like we might have an intruder on the grounds."

Houston groaned. What the hell else could go wrong today?

He stood, but then looked at Gabrielle and Jay. He didn't want to leave her alone with a man who might have shot himself in order to get to her. But he also didn't want to leave Jay unattended in the house. The man might try to go after Lucas. Or Gabrielle.

"Stand back from him," Houston instructed Gabrielle. He took out the gun and put it in her hand. "Keep him at gunpoint. I'll be right back."

Gabrielle glanced down at the gun. "Is this really necessary?"

"Unfortunately, yes."

She didn't argue. She simply gave a shaky nod, and even though Houston hated to leave her with this kind of dirty duty, he had to check out the possible intruder.

"Wait here with Gabrielle," Houston told Greta. Not that the maid would be much help if Jay was about to launch some kind of attack, but he might think twice if there were two instead of one.

Houston glanced at Gabrielle one last time, and then hurried down the hall to Dale's office. He spotted the surveillance screen used for the system, and he saw what the motion-activated cameras were recording. Someone was indeed climbing over the east fence.

Houston zoomed in on the images and cursed.

He took out his phone and called Sheriff Whitley. The man answered on the first ring.

"I was about to call you," he told Houston. "I had to cut Harlan Cordell loose about a half hour ago. He lawyered up, and there wasn't enough evidence to hold him."

"Yeah. I know. He's crawling over my fence as we speak."

Now it was the sheriff who cursed. "I have a deputy already on the way out there. He should arrive with the ambulance you requested through nine one one."

Good. But that could take twenty minutes or more. Houston watched as Cordell landed on the ground at the bottom of the fence. The man didn't hesitate. Cordell made a beeline for the house.

"Why do you need an ambulance?" the sheriff asked.

"Gabrielle's brother is here, too. He claims someone shot him. He'd definitely injured, but I can't tell if he did it himself or if someone did try to kill him."

"I'm on my way," the sheriff said, and he ended the call.

Houston wanted the sheriff on the scene, but he wouldn't arrive any faster than the deputy and the ambulance. By then, Cordell might have made it all the way to the house. Houston didn't intend to let that happen.

He took out his cell and pressed in the security code that Dale had installed to alert the ranch hands. Of course, when his foreman had put that security measure into place, he'd been thinking about flood or tornado warnings. Maybe even an attempted theft. He likely hadn't counted on someone like Cordell trespassing, and perhaps trying to commit a murder. Even if Cordell didn't have killing on his mind, there could be no good reason why he'd climb over the fence.

Had Cordell been the one to shoot Jay?

That was certainly one question Houston intended to ask the man.

He grabbed a handgun from Dale's desk and checked to make sure it was loaded. It was. Houston hurried back to the foyer and found things just as he'd left them. Gabrielle was still holding the Smith and Wesson on her brother, and Greta was waiting, her own cell phone poised in her hand as if she were ready to make an emergency call.

"Cordell's on the grounds," Houston told Gabrielle.

"Lanny?" Jay questioned, and he looked just as alarmed and stunned as his sister. "You're sure?"

"I'm sure," Houston insisted.

Despite her reaction to hearing about Cordell being on the grounds, Houston didn't have time to sugarcoat this. "I'm going after him. Lock the door when I leave, and make sure Jay stays put."

"I'm not the guilty party here," Jay grumbled. "Harlan Cordell is a dangerous man."

Houston ignored him and gave Gabrielle one last look before he disarmed the security alarm on the front door. "The sheriff, a deputy and the ambulance are all on the way."

"Then wait for them," Gabrielle pled. "Don't go after Cordell alone."

"I won't be alone. The ranch hands have all been alerted, and I'll grab one of them as my backup."

Gabrielle caught on to his arm. "Please, don't go out there."

Houston hated to see the fear and worry in her eyes, but he couldn't reassure her with just words or by staying put.

"If Cordell gets close enough to the house, he might fire shots through the windows," Houston said.

"Oh, God," Gabrielle mumbled. Obviously understanding now, she nodded. They couldn't risk a shooting, because Lucas might be hurt.

Houston brushed a kiss on her mouth and hurried out the door. Leaving was a huge risk, because Jay might indeed be up to something; but right now Cordell was the bigger risk, and he had to be neutralized.

Keeping his gun ready, Houston jumped in one of the work trucks that was parked at the back of the house.

"We have an intruder by the east fence," he shouted out the window to a pair of ranch hands who he saw near the stables. "I don't want this SOB to get anywhere near the house."

That got them moving, and they shouted out for others to assist. His men began to fan out around the yards and the property.

Houston started for the east fence, and he saw in his rearview mirror that a ranch hand from one of the barns got into a pickup, as well, probably so he could follow Houston. He didn't wait for the man. Houston sped ahead, making his way down the graveled pasture road.

He tried to put a choke hold on his fears for Gabrielle's safety, but it was hard to do, and he prayed he wasn't making a mistake by leaving her alone.

The road soon narrowed as Houston had known it would, but he didn't slow down. He raced the truck through the path until he saw the east fence. What he didn't see was Cordell, but the man couldn't have gotten far on foot.

Houston drove off the road and went toward a cluster of trees and shrubs. He kept watch all around him and behind. He could see the ranch hand when he made the same turn that Houston had taken.

But where the hell was Cordell?

Houston finally spotted some movement in the trees, and he slammed on the brakes. He barely took time for the truck to stop when he barreled out. He used the truck for cover so he could get a better look.

Cordell was there, just behind a sprawling live oak.

"I'm not armed!" Cordell shouted. "Don't shoot."

Of all the things he'd expected Cordell to say, that wasn't on Houston's list. He replayed the images he'd seen on the surveillance camera and knew he hadn't seen a gun in Cordell's hand, but he'd assumed he had a weapon tucked away.

And he probably did.

"Come out where I can see you," Houston instructed. "And put your hands in the air."

Much to Houston's surprise, Cordell did just that. He calmly lifted his hands and started out from the tree.

"I saw Jay," Cordell said, his voice a shout because of the distance between them. "I was on my way out of town, but then I saw him when he pulled into the ranch. I figured now was as good a time as any to collect that money he owes me."

"And you thought the best way to do that was to climb over the fence?"

Cordell shrugged. "He said he was getting the money from Mack Sadler. I didn't know if he was lying about that or not. If I'd called him, or if I'd driven right up in front of the house, Jay would have seen me and run. Or done something worse. Jay's more than a little desperate when it comes to seeing me."

Yeah. And Jay knew that Cordell was on the grounds because Houston had told him. Now, the question was, just how desperate was Jay to get away from Cordell, and to what extent would he go?

Houston glanced back at the ranch hand who was

making his way to them on foot. "Keep your gun on Cordell," Houston ordered. "When the sheriff gets here, I want Cordell arrested for trespassing." That might keep him away from the ranch until he at least made bail.

Houston got back in his truck, started it and hit the accelerator. He had to get back to Gabrielle because something was wrong. He could feel it in his gut.

He took out his cell and phoned the house. Normally, it was a line Dale would have answered, but since he wasn't there, Greta should have taken the call.

She didn't.

Four rings and finally Lily Rose picked up.

"Is everything okay there?" Houston couldn't get the question out fast enough.

"I think so. Gabrielle called me a few minutes ago and told me to stay put in my room with the baby. The door's locked, and I'll keep it that way until I hear from one of you."

That was good, but it wasn't good that Gabrielle hadn't answered the house phone—especially since there was an extension in the foyer. He cursed the fact that he didn't have her cell number with him, and he raced back toward the ranch house.

It seemed to take him hours to drive that mile or so back, and Houston's worst fears were confirmed when he finally reached the house.

Gabrielle and Greta weren't inside as they were supposed to be. They were on the porch. Gabrielle wasn't armed, but Jay certainly was.

Jay had the gun that Houston had given Gabrielle.

Chapter Twelve

Gabrielle had to stop this.

If she didn't, it could turn deadly in a hurry.

"Don't shoot!" she called out to Houston, when he jumped from his truck with his own gun aimed and ready to fire.

Houston was alone. No sign of Cordell, and she wasn't sure if that was good or bad. What was good was that Houston was in one piece and had come back safely.

Like Gabrielle, he was breathing heavily. He had sweat on his face. And she knew he wanted to know what was going on.

Gabrielle wasn't sure.

One minute, her brother had started to writhe in pain, and the next minute he'd grabbed the gun from her when she knelt beside him to check on his wound.

For an injured man in so much pain, Jay had moved extremely fast, and he'd snatched the gun from her hand, bolted from the floor and was out the door before she could catch up to him.

Now Jay had that gun aimed at his own head.

"I'm not hanging around so Harlan Cordell or Mack

Sadler can kill me," Jay shouted. "I won't just let them finish me off."

Gabrielle went down the steps toward her brother. She didn't break into a run because she didn't want to make any sudden moves that would startle him. She also didn't want to do anything to give the ranch hands or Houston a reason to fire. There were at least a half-dozen weapons trained on Jay, and this could end deadly in the blink of an eye.

"Cordell is being held by one of my men," Houston explained. "He's not here to kill you."

"Maybe not now. But it's just a matter of time." Jay wearily shook his head.

"Put down the gun," Gabrielle insisted, "and we can talk. You need medical attention."

"I need my sister to believe me!" Jay yelled. "And you can't or won't because Houston's already poisoned your mind against me."

"That's not true." Gabrielle tried to steady her breath, and she walked down another step. "Houston and I only want the truth. We want to protect Lucas."

"If that's what you want, then get the baby away from him." Jay tossed a glare at Houston. "Because he and his father are behind this. Can't you see that, Gabrielle? They're the ones you should be afraid of, not me."

"For all I know, Harlan Cordell could be the person behind this." She glanced at Houston again to make sure he was staying put. He was, thank God. But she had no idea how long that would last. She only had minutes or less, when she heard the sirens in the distance.

The ambulance and the deputy weren't far away.

Jay cursed when he heard the sound, and he jammed the gun even harder against his head.

"Don't go any closer," Houston warned Gabrielle, when she reached the last step.

"He's right, about *this* anyway," Jay fired back. "Don't come closer. Because if you do, I'll pull this trigger and you'll be responsible for killing me."

She froze, even though she wasn't convinced that Jay would indeed take his own life. Still, Gabrielle couldn't risk it. Maybe it was callous for her to feel this way about her own brother, but if he started shooting, the others might, too. And one of the bullets could hurt Lucas.

Gabrielle didn't intend to risk that for Jay, or for anybody.

Jay used his wounded arm to open the car door, and he didn't seem so wounded anymore. He got inside behind the steering wheel. Houston inched forward, but instead of going to her brother, she went to him.

"Let him go," Gabrielle told Houston. It was a risk, because Jay might still need medical attention, but it was better than his committing suicide.

When she made it to Houston, he looped his arm around her and pulled her behind his truck. Probably for cover, just in case her brother decided to start shooting. But he didn't. Jay started the car and sped away.

Gabrielle continued to hold her breath.

It was still possible that he'd run into the ambulance or the deputy. If not, he would likely head for the hospital. Maybe then he would get the help he needed.

With one crisis temporarily averted, she looked at Houston to make sure he was truly all right. He didn't seem harmed, so that was one prayer answered.

"Did you find Cordell?" she asked.

He nodded, but kept his attention fastened to Jay's car. "One of the ranch hands is keeping an eye on him until the sheriff arrives."

Good. That meant Cordell wasn't roaming around, ready to strike. One less worry. And at the moment, she needed as few worries as possible. When her brother had ripped that gun from her hand, her adrenaline had gone through the roof. For several terrifying moments, she had thought he was going to kill her and then go after Lucas. It might take her body a while to understand that hadn't been his intention. She was still shaking.

The moment Jay's car was out of sight, Houston caught on to her and got her moving back into the house. Gabrielle tried to thank him. She tried to tell him how sorry she was for allowing Jay to get his hands on the gun. But she couldn't seem to speak. The only thing she could do was stand there and tremble.

Houston pulled her into his arms and kissed her. "It's all right," he whispered. And he kept repeating it until it started to settle in.

They had both come through this unscathed…physically, anyway.

She looked up at him, ready now to give him that explanation about what had happened with her brother and the gun, but she heard Lucas cry. It was a sound she knew all too well. Her baby was hungry. And he wouldn't know or care about what had just happened. He simply wanted to nurse.

"Go to him," Houston said. "I need to talk to the sheriff, and then I'll be up."

She was functioning on autopilot now, so she nodded and headed up the stairs.

"It's me," Gabrielle said, when she knocked on her suite door.

Lily Rose was right there to open it, and she had a crying Lucas in her arms. Ready for Gabrielle. She took the baby, went to the love seat and started to nurse him.

Almost immediately, she felt the change in her body. Everything started to level out, and it got even better when she kissed her son's forehead and cheek. Holding Lucas was nothing short of a miracle, and she was thankful that he wasn't aware of any of the danger going on around him.

"You look like you've seen a ghost," Lily Rose told her. With her face obviously wearing her fear, the nanny sank down in the chair across from Gabrielle. "Is it over? Are we safe now?"

"I'm not sure," Gabrielle answered, honestly. And she had no idea what to do about that. If she left the ranch, the danger would no doubt just follow her. She knew that now.

"Then we're staying here?" Lily Rose asked.

Gabrielle didn't know the answer to that, either, but she probably needed to put some distance between Houston and her, just so she could try to think this through. Yes, she trusted him, but she trusted herself more, and she had to come up with the solution that was the safest and best for Lucas.

"I need to talk to Houston," Gabrielle said, to answer Lily Rose's question.

She finished nursing Lucas and moved him to her

shoulder so she could burp him. The baby immediately fell back asleep, so Gabrielle continued to pat and rub his back until he finally burped. Even though she wanted to sit and hold him longer, she also needed to get an update as to what was going on. Maybe by now, Jay had arrived at a hospital.

Gabrielle gently placed Lucas back in the crib and started for the door. The sound stopped her in her tracks, and it sent her heart to the floor.

Lily Rose gasped, because she no doubt recognized the sound, as well.

A gunshot.

It hadn't come from the house, or Gabrielle didn't think so, anyway. Still, her first thought was of Houston. Had someone shot at him again?

Or worse. Had the gunman succeeded this time?

"Watch the baby," Gabrielle told Lily Rose, and she threw open the door.

The first thing she saw was Houston making his way up the stairs toward them. There was no blood, thank God. And he didn't appear to be injured.

"Are you okay?" she immediately asked.

"I'm fine." He hooked his arm around her waist and pulled her back into the room. His gaze fired around to the windows, and he was obviously checking to make sure the curtains were closed.

They were.

And the crib was nowhere near the door or any of the glass. Houston had made the room as safe as possible, but Gabrielle didn't know if that was enough. Actually, she wasn't sure *anything* was enough right now.

"Who fired the shot?" Gabrielle wanted to know.

Houston shook his head. "I don't know yet. The sheriff's checking on it now." The words had no sooner left his mouth when his phone buzzed.

"It's Sheriff Whitley," Houston said to her.

Lucas stirred, fussing a bit, and Lily Rose went to him while Houston stepped back into the hall so he could take the call. Gabrielle stood there, trying to hear what had prompted the call, but whatever it was, it caused Houston's forehead to bunch up.

"You've got to be kidding me," he grumbled. He scrubbed his hand over his face and groaned before his gaze came to hers. "Cordell or maybe his henchman fired the shot."

"Cordell?" She shook her head. "I thought your ranch hand was holding him at gunpoint?"

"He was, until someone fired that shot. The sheriff arrived just as Cordell was getting away."

Gabrielle was almost afraid to ask. "And your ranch hand? Did Cordell shoot him?"

Houston held up his hand in a wait-a-second gesture, and he continued to listen to whatever else the sheriff was telling him. Several moments later, Houston hung up and put his phone away.

"The ranch hand is okay. The shot missed him." Houston shook his head. "Hell, it's possible the shot wasn't even intended to hit him. He said he dropped to the ground when he heard it."

"But Cordell fired it?"

Another head shake. "He doesn't know. Cordell jumped behind one of the trees just seconds before the shot was fired, so he could have been the one to pull the trigger. Or his accomplice could have climbed over the fence, as well. The alarm tripped again, but we don't know if Cordell did that as he was getting away, or if it was tripped when someone else came in."

"You have surveillance cameras, though," she reminded him.

"Yeah. And the sheriff and I both will want to take a look at the footage. Right now, my guess is that Cordell's henchman is responsible."

That made sense, too, because there had been two men in the car that had stopped in front of her brother's apartment. Maybe Cordell had had his henchman wait on the other side of the fence, and once Jay was gone, there was no reason for Cordell to hang around.

Houston went past her to the crib and looked down at Lucas. The baby had already drifted back to sleep. Still, Houston leaned down and kissed Lucas's cheek.

He turned back toward her. "The house is locked down," he said in a whisper. "No one in and no one out. I want it to stay that way until Cordell and your brother are in custody."

He gave a heavy sigh as if he expected her to disapprove of lumping her brother in the same company as Cordell. Old habits nearly made her do just that. But after what had happened today, Jay obviously needed some psychological help, along with treatment for the gunshot wound.

Houston checked the clock on the wall of the sitting area. It was already midafternoon. "You should eat something. I'll have Greta bring up a tray, and then I'll be in my office looking at that surveillance footage."

He headed for the door and Gabrielle followed him. "I

can help you with that," she insisted. She glanced back at Lily Rose. "Come and get me when Lucas wakes up."

The nanny assured her that she would, and Gabrielle trailed down the hall after Houston.

"You should get some rest," Houston suggested.

"So should you," she suggested right back, knowing that rest wouldn't happen. Not until they were sure Lucas was safe, and that wouldn't happen until they got to the bottom of who wanted them dead. The surveillance footage was a start. She hoped.

Houston gave her a thin smile—maybe his way of letting her know that he was glad she was there. Or maybe that was wishful thinking. Maybe the crazy attraction between them really was all he felt. And that was yet something else she would have to sort out when the time came.

They went to his office, which was as impressive as the rest of the house. In addition to the ebony-colored furniture and hobnail leather sofa, the room had a massive fireplace, and the walls were decorated with awards and such that the ranch had won because of their livestock and cutting horses. It was yet another reminder that Houston's cowboy roots ran deep and rich.

He had barely stepped inside his office when his phone buzzed again. Houston put the call on speaker and set the cell on his desk so he could turn on his computer.

"Houston," the caller greeted. "It's Jordan Taylor."

Gabrielle recognized the name. It was the security specialist that Houston had mentioned several times. That immediately grabbed her attention.

"You have something for me?" Houston asked.

"I do." And the man paused. "You asked me to find out if your father or your foreman, Dale Burnett, had any phone contact with Jay Markham. They did."

Houston groaned. "Which one?"

"Both."

That hung in the air for several moments, while, mentally, Gabrielle went through the conversation they'd had with her brother. Houston was no doubt doing the same. She'd assumed her brother was lying when he claimed that Mack had wanted to pay him to find her, but maybe it hadn't been a lie after all.

"I went through all the phone records for the ranch," Jordan continued, "and your father's calls to Markham started about four weeks ago."

Four weeks? Gabrielle pulled in her breath. That must have been about the time that Mack realized he couldn't find her on his own.

"And what about Dale Burnett's calls?" Houston questioned. "When did those happen?"

"Two days ago. He made three calls, all within the same hour. But I don't think he actually spoke to Markham. It appears the calls went straight to voicemail. Your father, on the other hand, was on the line long enough for the eleven calls he made that I can safely say that Markham and he had conversations," Jordan explained. "If I learn anything else, I'll let you know."

"Thank you," Houston mumbled. And he stabbed the End Call button.

"So Dale might be innocent," Gabrielle suggested. But she certainly couldn't say the same for Houston's father. Or her brother.

Houston bracketed his hands on his desk and stared up

at the oil painting above the fireplace. It was obviously a three-generation portrait, with Mack in the middle and flanked on the right by Houston and on the left by his own father.

Family.

And apparently Gabrielle and Houston could blame his family for some part in what had happened to her. Still, she didn't want to believe that Mack or Jay wanted to murder them.

"I was hoping Cordell would be the guilty party," she mumbled. "Or Salvador Franks."

"They might still be. But even if one of them is the main perpetrator, my father had a hand in this." He turned to her. "And I'm truly sorry about that."

"So am I." And she was surprised that she meant it. "For better or worse, that's Lucas's bloodline," she said, tipping her head to the painting. "His family," Gabrielle reluctantly added.

Houston stared at her, squinting a little, as if trying to figure out what she meant by that.

"I'm not just handing him over to you," she said, to clarify. "But I also know I can't keep him to myself."

That hurt more than she'd imagined it would. And she'd imagined the worse. For years, Gabrielle had planned for this child and the life she would have with him. That life didn't include sharing him with his biological father. But Houston was more than that. He loved Lucas, and even if it were within her power to take him and the Sadlers out of the picture, she couldn't do it.

She hadn't even realized she was crying, until she felt the hot tears on her cheeks. Gabrielle quickly swiped them away, but more followed.

Houston went to her and pulled her into his arms. "Shh," he whispered. "It's okay."

For some reason, those simple words and his gesture helped soothe her. Of course, after the day they'd had, her nerves were all over the place, and almost anything that didn't involve bullets or death threats probably would have soothed her.

She suddenly became aware of the close body contact between them. Specifically, his chest against hers. His thigh pressed hard against her leg. She also became aware of the rhythm of his breathing. His scent. And that face. There was always that face. She could dismiss some things about Houston, but his good looks weren't one of them.

Gabrielle pulled away. The attraction between them didn't have boundaries, and Houston and she had too much to do, to go at each other again as if they were teenagers ruled by their hormones.

Houston pulled her right back to him.

He looked down at her and their eyes met. That was it. That was all it took before Gabrielle found herself moving onto her tiptoes so she could kiss him.

So much for trying to fight this.

One touch of his mouth on hers, and she didn't want to fight it, anyway. Of course, she'd known it would happen. She was mindless when it came to Houston. So Gabrielle didn't try to stop herself when she wound her hands around his neck and pulled him down to her to make the body contact even closer.

He made a sound of pleasure, a rumble deep in his throat, but there seemed to be a question mark at the end of that sound. That was reasonable. It was sane to question this, but he didn't stop, and neither did Gabrielle.

It's just kisses, she told herself.

And for a few seconds that was true. They did just kiss; but it didn't take long for Houston to deepen those kisses. It also didn't take Gabrielle long before she wanted more. Houston's mouth had a unique way of taking her mind off the real world by setting her body on fire. And that's exactly what was happening now.

He moved, turning her, and pressing her against his desk. The new position created some interesting pressure at the juncture of her thighs, and she felt her body getting ready for something it thought it was going to get.

Just kisses, she mentally repeated.

Her grip tightened on the back of his neck. She could feel the need and the heat building, and each new kiss and touch only fueled that need.

Houston put his hands on her waist, moving her away from the desk and toward the door. She'd known this was coming. He was going to stop, and probably send her back to her room. He would put an end to this. Or not.

He made it across the room, their mouths still fused together, his hands all over her, and he reached behind them and locked the door.

"If you're going to say no," he mumbled against her mouth, "say it now."

She couldn't say no. She couldn't say anything. Gabrielle didn't have enough breath to speak. Besides, she didn't want this to stop. She wanted it to go exactly where it was already headed.

So she pulled Houston back to her and kissed him.

Chapter Thirteen

Houston figured he was a couple of steps past losing his mind, but he no longer cared. His body had jumped to the take-Gabrielle-now mode, and his brain was just going along for the ride.

Later, much later, he figured she would regret this, but he decided to give her something worth the regret.

Something they'd both remember.

With the door locked, Houston maneuvered Gabrielle back across the room and toward the sofa. It wasn't an ideal place to make love to her, but it would have to do. Neither time nor location was on their side here, and it wouldn't be long before his phone buzzed or someone came looking for them. Truth was, things were falling apart fast. But the only thing he wanted to think about right now was Gabrielle.

He kissed her—much too hard—and he handled her as if this were a routine quickie between two old lovers who were still starved for each other. Houston reminded himself to slow down, to take it easy with her, but that reminder went south when she pulled his shirt from his jeans and ran her hands over his bare stomach and chest.

Oh, man. The woman sure knew how to make him burn.

They landed in a tumble on the sofa, with their arms and legs all wound around each other. And with him on top of her. The kissing didn't stop. Neither did those mind-blowing caresses she was doing to his chest.

Houston did some caressing of his own. He ran his hand along the outside of her right thigh until he reached the zipper of her jeans. He touched her there through the fabric, and he heard her make that sound of pure pleasure as she lifted her hips to make intimate contact.

He was sunk.

The kissing became more frantic. So did the touches. Her sounds of pleasure became ones of demand. It was a demand that Houston was feeling, too, and he knew this wouldn't last long enough for any real foreplay. If he got the chance to be with her again, he promised himself he'd do better. But for now, he just wanted relief from the heat that was building inside both of them.

Gabrielle fought with his shirt and got it unbuttoned. Thankfully, her top was stretchy, so he just shoved it up and unhooked her bra so that her breasts pressed against his chest. It was a mind-searing sensation, but there wasn't time to enjoy it, because Gabrielle went for his zipper.

He caught her by the wrist so he could undo her jeans first. She fought and squirmed against him. But Houston didn't give up. He slid his hand into her jeans. Into her panties. And he touched her the way he'd wanted to touch her since he'd first laid eyes on her.

She was hot, wet and ready, and that sent all kinds of signals to his body and brain to get on with this. Still, he managed to slide his fingers into that wet heat, and he got to see what his touch was doing to her when he looked into her eyes. The passion was there, glazing through all those shades of brown, and she made that yearning sound again.

It was time.

Houston released her wrist, and Gabrielle didn't waste a second. She went after his zipper. He went after her jeans. And while it wasn't pretty, they did manage to get off most of their clothes. Well, the necessary ones anyway.

And he left her for a few painful seconds while he located a condom in his desk drawer. He didn't want to know how long it'd been there, he only wanted protection and he wanted it fast.

He did rein in some of his passion, though, when he pushed inside her. Houston reminded himself that she'd had a baby only six weeks earlier, but Gabrielle showed no signs of pain. Just the opposite. She wrapped her legs around his and drew him deep into her.

Houston had to take a moment to deal with the blinding pleasure that speared through him, but Gabrielle obviously didn't want to waste another second. She lifted her hips, forcing the friction and the intimate contact that would bring this to a climax way too soon.

Of course, an hour would have been way too soon for Houston.

Still, he gave into what their bodies were demanding, and he moved with her. Despite the awkwardness of their undressing, they fell into a rhythm that was just what they needed.

It was perfect. Houston moving inside her. Gabrielle

urging him on with those slight adjustments she made with each thrust.

Because he was watching her, Houston knew when she got close to the edge. And he gave her what she needed to push her over.

Gabrielle said his name. Her voice was low and hoarse. Hardly more than a whisper. But it roared through him as if she had shouted it. And it was all Houston needed to fly over that edge with her.

He gathered her into his arms, keeping her close, while they both came back down to earth. Her breaths came fast and heavy. So did his. And he could hear his own heartbeat in his ears. All normal, considering they'd just had sex.

But it didn't exactly feel normal. It felt better than that. It felt *right*.

That caused him to shake his head. What he felt for Gabrielle shouldn't be this deep and this strong. But it was. Somehow, he'd made the leap from physical attraction to wondering if he should be doing something to make this more permanent.

Except it was too soon for that. Wasn't it?

Probably. After all, he hadn't worked out what his intentions were toward her. Yes, he cared. Yes, he had the hots for her. However, he didn't know how much of that intensity had to do with the fact that she'd given birth to Lucas and how much of it was just because she was a damn attractive woman.

"Don't overthink this," Gabrielle said.

Houston looked down at her and realized she was staring up at him.

"It was just sex," she added.

That clarified things for him. Sort of. It certainly clarified that she wasn't looking for anything that involved a leap to a permanent relationship.

She cupped his face, kissed him, and then moved in such a way to let him know that she wanted to get up. Houston got off her, and Gabrielle immediately stood. She started to gather up her clothes. What she didn't do was look at him.

"Don't overthink this," she repeated.

He agreed with that, until he saw her stepping into her white lace panties. And Houston wanted her all over again. *Oh, yeah*.

He was in trouble, and *under*thinking it wouldn't help.

Gabrielle used the adjoining bathroom to freshen up and finish dressing, and when she came out, Houston changed places with her and did the same.

"We should, uh, start looking at the surveillance footage," she reminded him, after he came back into his office.

Houston agreed, and he might have jumped right into if she hadn't made that "uh" hesitation. He went to her and pulled her into his arms.

"We probably should talk about it." He brushed a kiss on her forehead.

"It won't help," she insisted, pushing away from him. Gabrielle put her hands on her hips and stared at him. "We knew this was going to happen."

"Yeah," he agreed. "But I don't think we expected it to be that good."

He waited, figuring she might try to refute that, but

she huffed and shook her head. "I can't fall this hard for you, Houston."

For some dumb reason, that made him smile. "I was thinking the same thing about you."

That only made her look more annoyed. "This is about Lucas. Mentally, we're trying to work out how best to handle the situation with him."

Houston didn't disagree, though he could have. But for now, maybe it was a good thing that they still had some issues with each other. Some hesitation. Some *uh's.*

If not for those things, he'd be hauling her right back onto that sofa for round two.

Instead, he loaded the surveillance footage and got to work.

Because she still looked tired and hungry, Houston called the kitchen and requested some trays be brought up for Lily Rose, as well as for Gabrielle and him. He also had Gabrielle sit at his desk, and he stood behind her, controlling the speed and the angle of the images with a remote control.

They were only minutes into the task when Houston's cell buzzed. With all the craziness going on at the ranch, he expected the call to be from the sheriff. It wasn't. It was from his father.

Great. Just what he didn't need.

Houston considered not answering, but it was possible that Mack knew something about what was going on. Hell, it was possible that Mack was the *reason* things were happening as they were.

"This better be important," Houston greeted.

"It is. I just heard about all the trouble that went on at the ranch, what with Jay and all. Are you okay?"

"Fine. But if that's all you wanted to ask—"

"It's not," Mack insisted, before Houston could hang up. But he didn't explain himself right away. His father hesitated for several seconds. "Look, I know this is probably something you don't want to hear right now, but I don't think you should be trusting either Gabrielle or her brother."

"Funny, Jay said the exact same thing about you."

"Well, he would, wouldn't he? He wants to drive a wedge between us, and he's succeeding. Houston, the man just wants money, and he doesn't care who he uses to get it."

Houston didn't doubt that for a minute. However, he could take objection to something his father had said. "But why do you lump Gabrielle in with Jay as someone I shouldn't be trusting?"

She glanced back at him, and Houston placed his hand on her shoulder, hoping to reassure her that he wasn't about to throw her under a bus.

"She's always stuck up for him," Mack said.

"Not this time. Gabrielle and I are putting Lucas first. That means she's not trusting her brother, and I'm not trusting you—until we have proof that neither of you is behind the attempts to kill us."

"I wouldn't kill you," Mack insisted. "Yeah, I've made some mistakes, and I'm sorry for them. I'm sorry I didn't tell you about Gabrielle getting Lizzy's embryo. I'm especially sorry that I tried to get the baby from her. But I'm not sorry you have a son."

Neither was Houston. But being happy about Lucas and forgiving his father were two different things.

"Just watch your back, son," Mack added. "And after

you learn the truth, I'll be right here, waiting. Because there's nothing you can say or do to me that would make me stop loving you."

Houston didn't return the sentiment. He hung up and gave his full attention to the images that were scrolling across the computer screen.

"Your father might be right," Gabrielle mumbled.

Surprised, Houston raised his eyebrows. "About what?"

"My brother." She swiveled the chair around to face him. "I looked at Jay's wound when he was here, and it was superficial."

Houston nodded. He'd noticed the same thing. "You think he could have shot himself?"

She shrugged. "He might have thought it was the only way I'd let him onto the ranch. And he was right. If he'd just showed up, I wouldn't have let him in. He's desperate for money, and when he's this desperate, I think he's capable of almost anything."

It was that "almost" part that was giving Houston the most trouble. Jay and Cordell wanted money, and that was a powerful motive for attempted murder. Of course, Salvador Franks had a reputation to salvage. He might even be facing some jail time and would want to cover up the mistakes that had been made at the Cryogen Clinic.

But where did his father fit in?

Houston could perhaps see Mack trying to eliminate Gabrielle, but he couldn't see his father doing that with Houston in the car with her. Or maybe he was giving his father too much credit.

Was he being blind to Mack's involvement the very

way he'd originally accused Gabrielle of being blind to Jay's guilt? Possibly.

Maybe Mack had given up on Houston being the Sadler heir, and had pinned all his hopes on Lucas. It was a long shot. Well, it was, as far as Houston was concerned, but he couldn't dismiss that his father might have already mapped out a future with his grandson—at Houston's own expense. With Houston out of the way, Mack wouldn't have any obstacles in his path to go after Gabrielle.

She moved closer to the laptop screen, her attention nailed to the images there. That caused Houston to do the same. He saw Cordell hiding behind the trees, and he slowed down the speed so he wouldn't miss anything.

"You must have already been on your way back to the house," Gabrielle pointed out.

She was right, because Houston saw the ranch hand he'd left to keep an eye and a gun on Cordell. He also saw something else.

Houston adjusted the angle, zooming in on some movement on the left side of the screen. Movement around the area of the fence.

"Someone was there," Gabrielle mumbled.

Definitely.

Houston tried to get a better picture, but because the person was out of range, his image was blurry. A moment later, the person ducked out of sight. So Houston reversed the feed in order to get a better look.

Gabrielle inched closer to the screen. "I think it's a man."

So did he. Houston froze the best frame he could find, and he moved closer, as well. Even though he couldn't make out the person's features, he could see the colors of the clothes he was wearing. Clothes that he immediately recognized.

Hell. What was *he* doing there?

Chapter Fourteen

Gabrielle waited, her attention divided between a very alert Lucas and Houston, who had his cell pressed to his ear while he paced across the floor of her suite.

Houston volleyed glances between Lucas and her, and while he seemed on the verge of a smile whenever his attention landed on Lucas, his face was tight with anger and concern.

Dale was the reason for this latest round of that concern.

Even though Gabrielle hadn't immediately recognized the man's clothes on the surveillance footage they'd been watching, Houston certainly had, and he'd been trying to speak to Dale for the past six hours. He'd left plenty of messages but hadn't managed to talk to the man.

"No luck," Houston mumbled, shutting his phone. "I keep getting a recording that says he's out of the service area."

Which could mean nothing. There were plenty of dead zones in the countryside and even around the ranch. Besides, the person on the surveillance footage could be someone who wanted to make them think it was Dale.

Mack, maybe. Or it could have even been Salvador or some unknown accomplice there to help Cordell.

The one person she knew it wasn't was Jay. At the time of the footage, he'd been lying in the foyer at the house. Probably with a fake wound and the hope that he could milk Houston or Mack for some money.

Houston put away his phone and came back to the bed where she was lying with Lucas. Gabrielle was on her side, facing the baby. Houston climbed onto the bed next to Lucas.

"I've never seen him this alert," Houston commented, and he caught on to the baby's tiny toes as Lucas kicked.

"It won't last," Gabrielle said. "He usually falls asleep within a half hour after nursing." And since it'd already been fifteen minutes since he'd finished his dinner, he wouldn't stay awake much longer.

Lucas pursed his mouth, but then flinched when he made a loud cooing sound. Both Gabrielle and Houston laughed.

Gabrielle risked looking at Houston, figuring there would be more awkwardness between them, but it wasn't there. They were just two people marveling at the miracle of a newborn.

"Have you thought about getting married?" Houston asked.

She nearly choked on her own breath. "W-hat?"

"Married," he said, as if that clarified everything. He calmly continued to run his fingers across Lucas's toes.

Gabrielle opened her mouth, then closed it while

she rethought how she should respond to that. "Is that a proposal?" she finally settled for asking.

Houston shrugged, then nodded. "What if it was?"

She sat up. "Well, it wasn't much of one," she told him.

Houston frowned and seemed genuinely hurt. "I wasn't sure I should even ask."

"Then you shouldn't have." She couldn't help it. That riled her. "Houston, I'm not looking for a husband. Especially not one who feels obligated to marry me for the sake of my son. Lucas and I can get along just fine without my having a wedding ring on my finger."

"I didn't say you couldn't." His gaze came back to hers. Then he shook his head. "I don't know what I'm saying. I just know that we have to work out something, and after what happened in my office, I thought marriage might be a reasonable solution."

"'A reasonable solution,'" Gabrielle repeated. She gave him a flat look. "When and if I marry, there will be only one reason—because I'm in love with a man and he's in love with me." She paused. Waited.

Houston didn't answer.

"That's what I thought," she concluded, sounding snippier than she meant to. "You're not in love with me."

"I didn't say that," he snapped back.

He looked ready to launch into an argument, and Gabrielle was too tired for that, so she decided to nip it in the bud. "If and when you fall in love with me, and when and if I fall in love with you, then we'll discuss marriage."

But she didn't intend to settle for anything less than

love. If she'd learned anything over the past few days, it was that life was too short, and that she deserved more than just a "reasonable solution."

Now, the question was, was she ready to surrender her heart to Houston?

Thankfully, she didn't have to answer that, because his phone buzzed again. He took it from his pocket and pulled in his breath. "It's Dale."

He moved off the bed but put the call on speaker.

"I was over at my dad's place," Dale said. "No phone service out there, but I just listened to your messages."

"And?" Houston prompted, when Dale didn't continue.

"And you were right. I was there at the fence."

Houston groaned and mumbled some profanity. The tension in the room was suddenly thick and dark, in contrast to the soft sounds that Lucas was making.

"Why?" Houston demanded.

"Well, it wasn't to help Cordell, that's for sure. But I'm guessing that's what you think."

"I don't know what to think. That's why I want to know why you were there."

"When I left the ranch, I saw a car parked near one of the trails by the fence. I got out and had a look. That's when I spotted Zeke Dawkins, the ranch hand. And I also saw Cordell. He pulled a gun from the back of his pants and he fired into the air."

"Into the air?" Houston questioned.

"Yeah. He definitely wasn't aiming at anyone. But I didn't have a gun with me so I ran back to my truck to get the one I keep in the glove compartment. By the time

I got back, Cordell was gone, and Zeke was hightailing it back toward the ranch. I went after Cordell."

Houston met her gaze as if trying to judge her reaction, but Gabrielle had no idea what to make of Dale's story. It could be true. Maybe the ranch hand hadn't seen him, and that's why he hadn't said anything.

Still, she wasn't ready to trust Dale just yet.

"I don't suppose you found Cordell?" Houston asked.

"No. I lost him. I went looking for him up the trail. And I guess he doubled back, because a couple of minutes later I heard him drive away."

"Any reason you didn't call me and tell me about this?"

"I called one of the deputies. I didn't think you wanted to hear from me just yet."

Convenient that he'd phoned the deputy, and he almost certainly did, since that was something Houston would confirm. But again, it didn't mean Dale was telling the truth.

"Houston, I'm on your side," Dale told him.

Houston scrubbed his fingers hard over his forehead. "I want to believe that. I really do."

"Well, until you do, I'll stay away from the ranch."

Dale hung up, leaving Gabrielle with a bad feeling. If he was truly innocent, then Houston and she had some fences to mend with the man. However, it wasn't the time for that. There were too many unanswered questions.

Despite everything that was going on, Gabrielle yawned. She couldn't help it. She was exhausted, and the large dinner she'd eaten an hour earlier had only zapped more of her energy.

Houston obviously didn't miss the yawn, because he leaned over and gave her a peck on the cheek. "Why don't you get some sleep and I'll give Lucas a tour of the house?"

It was both tempting and a little alarming. Yes, she needed sleep, but part of her still wanted to hold on to Lucas, to make sure he would always be hers. A tour of the house wasn't likely to change that, but with every passing moment, Houston and Lucas were getting closer.

"It's just a tour," Houston assured her, as if reading her mind. He gently picked up Lucas and snuggled him into the crook of his arm. "Sleep," he insisted.

She had another thirty-second debate with herself and finally surrendered to the fatigue. Gabrielle kicked off her shoes and pulled the comforter over her.

"Don't be long," she told him.

Houston smiled, kissed Lucas and headed out the door.

Gabrielle was actually thankful for the bone-weary exhaustion, because with everything happening, she would have been a basket case if she could have mustered enough emotion for a real reaction. As it was, she couldn't even fight sleep for a solid minute. She felt her eyelids immediately drift closed.

They didn't stay closed.

The sound hummed through the estate and brought her off the bed. It wasn't a bullet or anything human. Just the mechanical hum of some kind of alarm. Her first thought was that it was a smoke detector. Her next thought was if there was a fire, she needed to get to Lucas.

Gabrielle hurried to the suite door, but Houston opened it before she could get to it.

"Is there a fire?" she immediately asked.

Houston shook his head and handed her the baby. "That's the security alarm. It means we might have an intruder."

HOUSTON DIDN'T EVEN try to reassure Gabrielle that everything was okay, or that maybe one of the employees or ranch hands could have tripped the alarm. He could tell from the look on her face that she knew the security alarm could mean the person who'd tried to kill them had just broken in.

Once Gabrielle had the baby out of his arms, Houston moved them back into the suite. "Who's there?" he called out, hoping it would be Greta who answered.

But Greta had probably already left after she'd prepared the dinner trays for them. Despite the size of the ranch, there normally was no full-time inside help. No one except for Dale.

But his foreman shouldn't be anywhere on the grounds, and especially not in the house, after Houston had put him on paid leave.

"Anyone there?" Houston tried again. No one answered.

Worse, the security system alarm probably wasn't loud enough for any of the ranch hands to hear it from their quarters on the other side of the barn. When the system had been set up, Houston hadn't considered that he might need outside help. He'd figured the alarm would alert his father, the security company, Dale and him to a possible burglary or fire. But alerting the occupants of the house was no longer enough. With Lucas and Gabrielle around, he needed more.

That meant he had to call someone for backup. Houston shut the door and reached for his phone. The screen lit up, but he saw the two words that sent his heart to his knees.

No Service.

That shouldn't happen in the house itself.

"What's wrong?" Gabrielle moved Lucas to her shoulder while she tried to soothe him.

"I'm not sure, but I think someone's jamming the phone." He hurried to the house phone in Gabrielle's sitting room and got the same result. The phone line was dead.

Since there weren't any storms in the area, and since they had electrical power, his theory about the jamming was probably right. And that meant they could be in big trouble.

He cursed himself for not doing more to protect his son. He shouldn't have waited for something like this to happen. But then, he'd never been in this kind of situation before.

There was a frantic knock at the door, and a moment later Lily Rose rushed in. "What's happening?"

"Someone might have broken in," Gabrielle answered.

Houston stopped and listened, hoping he'd hear a friendly voice or at least a familiar one. He didn't. And he couldn't take the chance that they'd be safe just waiting around to see what this alarm tripper would do next.

"I have to get a gun," he told them. He hated to leave

them alone for even a second, but he needed a way to defend them. There were several weapons in the house, and the nearest one was in his bedroom.

Houston looked out into the hall and didn't see anyone. But then, most of the lights were off. He also didn't hear any footsteps or sounds to indicate a person might be running up the stairs toward them. Still, he couldn't take the chance that it might happen.

"Come with me," he ordered.

He stepped out, had a closer look around and got them moving toward his bedroom. He moved them inside, shut the door and locked it.

"Try the phone again," he told Lily Rose. "Try to dial nine one one."

While the nanny did that, Houston went to the nightstand to take out his gun. He didn't have any spare ammunition, only what was loaded in the gun. That might not be enough. He hated to think of getting into a gun battle with Lucas and Gabrielle in the house, but he might not have a choice.

"The phone isn't working," Lily Rose said.

Houston mentally cursed.

"What should we do?" Gabrielle whispered. She had Lucas against her chest and shoulder and was patting his back.

"First, I need to find out who's in the house. And then, I have to get another gun and more ammunition. That means I have to go down the hall to my office."

Her eyes widened, and she drew in her breath. But then she nodded. "What about Lucas?"

Houston was on the same page with her. Their son had to come first. He glanced around, trying to come up with a plan. On the top of his list, he had to get Lucas into a safer area. There were too many windows in his room, and even though there might be an intruder inside, that didn't mean someone wasn't outside, as well.

Someone armed and ready to fire.

"Take Lucas to the bathroom and lock the door," he told Lily Rose. Houston waited until the nanny had done that before he motioned to the laptop on a corner desk. "Boot it up and click onto the security icon. You might be able to see if anyone is inside because there are some security cameras in the foyer and the sunrooms."

Though it was a long shot that an intruder would be in one of those three places. The house had twenty-seven rooms, and that meant there was plenty of space to hide and not be in camera range.

Houston pressed the gun into her hand.

Gabrielle frantically shook her head. "You'll need this if you're going out into the hall to get to your office."

Houston couldn't dispute that. He might need it. But Gabrielle might need it more as a last line of defense. "I want you to lock the door, and if anyone other than me tries to get it, you might have to shoot. Understand?"

She glanced at the gun and then at him. "I understand."

Good. Because he didn't have time to try to calm her fears. He needed to get the items from his office and then return so he could protect them.

Houston did take the extra second or two to brush a kiss on her mouth, and he hurried to the door. He peered out, bracing himself in case there was an attack, but he saw no one. There were still no sounds, either, and that made him hope that this was all some kind of malfunction with both the phones and the security system.

But Houston didn't really believe that.

Something was wrong.

He stepped into the hall and waited until Gabrielle had locked the door before he started for his office. It wasn't far, just six rooms away, but it suddenly felt as if he had miles to go. He grabbed a small marble statue from the hall table. Not that it would be much of a weapon against an armed intruder, but it was better than nothing.

Houston hurried but he didn't run. He didn't want the sound of his own footsteps drowning out anyone who might be close. Unfortunately, close could be many different places, because the U-shaped hall meant someone could be on the other side, making their way toward him. He hoped he would run into whoever this was, because it was better than the alternative—the guy sneaking up the stairs to Houston's suite where Gabrielle and Lucas were.

He paused when he got to the back of the hall and glanced around the corner. Empty. *Thank God.*

He glanced back at his suite, knowing that once he rounded the corner, it would be out of sight. That's why he had to make every second count.

Houston took a deep breath, raced up the back of the hall and practically dove across the space and into his open office door. But he didn't go all the way into the room. He turned on the lights and listened to make sure he had the place to himself. It was hard to hear over the buzz of the security system. The buzz was like white noise, muting everything else around him.

Like the rest of the house, his office had a lot of hiding

spaces, and he didn't want to be ambushed. Gabrielle, Lily Rose and Lucas needed him to get back to them safely.

When he was satisfied that no one was going to jump out at him, Houston went to his desk and took out the handgun he kept there. He scooped up some extra ammunition and stuffed it into his pockets. He hoped like hell he wouldn't need it.

Houston used the security system panel in his office to turn off the annoying alarm buzz. The silence was instant, practically closing in around him. And it was because of the silence that he heard the sound.

He'd already started for the office door, but he stopped, wondering if it was a sound he could dismiss. Even if it wasn't, he had to get moving. He had to get back to Gabrielle.

Houston glanced out the doorway of his office. This part of the hall was still empty, so he headed out, trying to keep watch. Trying to listen. And most of all, trying to hurry.

He heard the sound again. A thump, as if someone had bashed into something. It hadn't come from the front of the house, or even near his office. The sound had come from the direction of his suite.

Oh, hell.

Houston raced toward the sound, and he prayed that nothing was wrong. That it was just the wind.

But it wasn't. He heard something that turned his blood to ice. Gabrielle screamed out his name.

Chapter Fifteen

Gabrielle barely had time to boot up Houston's laptop when she heard the doorknob rattle. For such a small movement, it did huge things to her. Her breath and her thoughts began to race.

"Houston?" she softly called out. Nothing.

But she assured herself that it was possible he hadn't heard her over the buzzing sound of the security alarm.

Gabrielle picked up the gun from where she'd placed it on the desk, and she tiptoed toward the door. She only made it two steps when the alarm stopped. Just like that, it was quiet again, and she started to believe that she hadn't heard the doorknob after all.

She waited, listening. Or rather, trying to listen over the sound of her own pulse pounding in her ears. But the only thing she heard were the soft cooings that Lucas was making in the bathroom. Her son was obviously in a playful mood, and she couldn't be with him because there might be a threat.

"Houston?" she tried again, keeping her voice barely above a whisper.

She didn't want to alert Lily Rose. Or give away her

location if there was indeed the threat that her body was bracing itself for.

Still nothing.

She turned to go back to the laptop, but the doorknob rattled again. This time she knew it wasn't her imagination. Someone was on the other side.

"Who is it?" she called out, her voice louder now.

The person still didn't answer, but the doorknob shook almost violently.

Oh, God.

Was someone trying to break in?

A second later, Gabrielle got the answer to that question when there was a loud bash. Someone had rammed hard into the door.

She barely choked back a gasp, and she aimed the gun at the door.

"Who's out there?" she demanded.

Lucas stopped cooing, and she no longer heard Lily Rose's soft murmurings, which were no doubt meant to keep Lucas entertained and calm. Everything seemed to freeze.

Until the person bashed against the door again. Whoever it was, they were trying to break it down, and they weren't giving up.

"I have a gun," Gabrielle managed to say.

And she would use it. There was no way she would let the danger get to her son.

The next bash was harder and louder, and the wood around the jamb seemed to groan when it gave way. The door practically burst right at her and hit her. It slammed her into the wall, throwing her off-balance.

She didn't fire right away. She couldn't. The gun

slipped in her hand, and she had to reposition it before she could take aim. Besides, Gabrielle wanted to make sure it wasn't Houston, though she couldn't figure out why he wouldn't have answered her when she called out, and he almost certainly wouldn't have broken down the door.

She caught just a glimpse of someone wearing dark clothes and a ski mask, and then the gloved hand reached out and slapped off the lights, plunging them into darkness.

It wasn't Houston. The person dove right at her. And Gabrielle heard herself scream.

She called out Houston's name. But it was already too late. She couldn't get the gun ready and aimed before the person slammed right into her. Unlike the door, this jolt was hard because it hit her directly in the chest, and it knocked the breath right out of her.

Gabrielle dropped to the floor because she had no choice. The person's momentum caused her to fall, and her head smacked into a chair. It was nearly impossible to see because of the darkness, and that didn't help.

Her vision blurred. She fought with her breath, trying to gather enough air into her lungs so she could do something about this attack. But the person didn't give her a chance to get her bearings. He was on her before she could do anything.

And it was a *he*. There was no doubt about that. Gabrielle felt the corded muscles on his chest.

"Are you okay?" Lily Rose called out.

Gabrielle wanted the nanny to stay quiet, but it was probably a normal reaction. After all, Lily Rose had heard her scream.

The man hauled Gabrielle off the floor and shoved her in front of him. She still couldn't catch her breath—still couldn't see. But she could certainly feel. His rough grip on her shoulder and arm was bruising, and he wasn't gentle, either, when he jammed the gun against her right temple.

Oh, mercy.

Was she about to be executed? She thought of Lucas. If she died, then that only left Houston to protect him. Could he get there in time? Or had he even heard her? Her heart broke at the thought of this monster with the gun getting anywhere near her son.

But anger soon replaced that feeling of heartbreak. Neither Lucas nor she had done anything wrong, and they didn't deserve this.

Gabrielle nursed that anger, and she let it fuel her while she gathered the breath and strength she needed for a fight. She couldn't wait for Houston or anyone to save her. She might be the only thing standing between this man and her son.

Knowing it was a risk, she drew back her elbow so she could try to ram it into his stomach. But she stopped when she heard the footsteps in the hall, just outside the door.

Houston!

With his gun aimed, Houston stepped into the doorway. Even though it was dark, she could still see his intense expression. He glanced around the room, probably to make sure Lucas wasn't anywhere in the line of fire.

"Drop your gun," Houston ordered her attacker.

Gabrielle braced herself for the man to shoot her. But

he didn't. He also didn't respond to Houston's demand, other than to shove her forward several inches. What was he doing? Better yet, who *was* he?

All of their suspects were male, all about the same height, so she had no idea if this was Mack, Dale, Salvador Franks or Harlan Cordell. Or her brother.

But Gabrielle didn't want to believe that Jay would be willing to take things this far.

"You don't have to do this," Houston called out. "Just let Gabrielle go and tell me what you want. If it's money, I'll get it for you."

Still no verbal response.

But the man muscled her forward until she was only about five feet away from Houston. Part of her was glad they might be getting out of the suite. The more space between Lucas and the guns, the better. However, she did want to know what this man intended to do with Houston and her.

Gabrielle looked Houston straight in the eyes. "If he shoots, kill him," she instructed.

Houston's jaw muscles turned to iron. He didn't want her to die, but he probably realized he might not have a say in that matter. After all, she had a gun pointed directly at her head. At point-blank range, she wasn't likely to survive. But Houston would. And without her in the way, he would have a clean shot. A shot that Gabrielle wanted him to take.

"Let…her…go," Houston said, turning that icy stare to her attacker.

However, instead of doing that, the man pushed her forward even more. He dug the barrel of the gun even harder into her skin, but he let go of her arm. Gabrielle started to bolt forward, but the man turned the gun…on Houston.

She froze, waiting to see what he intended to do. But he didn't shoot. He took something from his pocket and thrust it forward. When Houston didn't take it, the man threw it at him. Houston dodged it, and she saw the folded sheet of paper flutter to the floor.

The man put the gun back to her head, and he curved his arm around her waist. Houston didn't take his gaze off her, and he didn't lower his gun when he bent down and picked up the paper. He glanced at it, his attention volleying between it and her as he scanned over whatever was written there.

Houston crammed the paper into his front jeans pocket. "No deal," he told the man.

Oh, God. What did that mean?

What had the man asked Houston to do? Judging from the fire that shot through Houston's eyes, it had something to do with Lucas.

The man's grip on her tightened, and he used that grip to maneuver her closer to Houston, inch by inch. Because Gabrielle didn't know what he had in mind, she struggled, trying to hold her ground, but it didn't do any good. They moved so close to Houston that he had to back up.

"I'll give you what you want now," Houston said. "But Gabrielle doesn't leave. She stays here."

The man didn't answer, but Gabrielle could feel his muscles tighten, and he was breathing way too fast. She hoped he was on the verge of hyperventilating, but she doubted they'd get that lucky.

Houston backed up more, probably because he knew each step would take them away from Lucas.

Gabrielle kept eye contact with Houston and tried to focus on each step and each little movement. All she needed was a distraction or something, and she might be able to break free.

Houston moved to the side when the man started down the stairs with her. Her captor turned, keeping her in front of them, while they walked backwards. That way, he could keep the gun on her while watching Houston, to make sure he didn't launch himself at them.

She wobbled, testing her balance and the man's reaction, but he only jammed the gun even harder against her skin. She glanced over her shoulder, behind them, and saw there were only about six more steps to go. Time was running out.

Once they reached the last step—which wasn't far away at all—Gabrielle figured that would be her best chance. She certainly didn't want to risk him getting her out of the house and into a vehicle. If that happened, God knows where he'd take her. Or what he would do to her.

Was this about Lucas? Or was did it have to do with what had happened at the Cryogen Clinic? If she could just get a look at her captor's face, then she would likely know the answer to that.

She counted each step until they reached the bottom one. And she knew it was time. Gabrielle took a deep breath and tried to convey to Houston what she was about to do. Not that it would help. He already had his gun aimed, and he'd bracketed his right wrist with his left hand.

If he got a shot, he would take it.

Gabrielle moved with the man when he stepped down onto the foyer floor, and she tried to give no indication to him as to what she was about to do. She said a quick prayer.

And threw all her weight backwards. She rammed right into him. At best, she was hoping to put him off-balance long enough for her to get away. But the *at best* didn't happen. Gabrielle felt herself falling backwards.

Just as the shot blasted from the man's gun.

HOUSTON DOVE TO THE SIDE, though he didn't have much room to dodge the bullet. His brain barely had time to register that the guy had missed when Houston saw him take aim again. At Gabrielle.

She fell to the floor, just barely out of the way, and definitely not out of the line of fire. Houston had to do something to get the shooter's attention off her and onto him.

Houston jumped over the side of the banister and landed on his feet on the marble floor. He pivoted so he could take aim at their attacker, but the guy ducked down and tried to grab on to Gabrielle. She kicked at him and tried to get away, and by doing so, she blocked the path so that Houston couldn't get a clean shot. He couldn't risk firing, because he might hit Gabrielle.

She got to her feet and ran into a formal sitting room. No lights were on in that particular room, but Houston didn't need the lights to see that she was about to be shot.

With Gabrielle out of the way, Houston fired at the man. He missed. The bullet left Houston's gun at the exact second the man bolted into the room after Gabrielle.

There was another shot. Houston cursed because the shot had come from the gunman. The SOB had no doubt fired at Gabrielle.

Leaving the meager cover of the stair banister, Houston went after them, but he knew he couldn't just fire at random. Lily Rose and Lucas were just one floor above, and he had no idea if the ceilings would be able to block bullets. And he couldn't risk it.

With his gun ready, Houston paused at the arched opening of the sitting room, and he peered around the corner. He didn't see anyone, but there was a lot of bulky furniture for someone to hide behind. He hoped that's exactly what Gabrielle was doing—hiding. He needed her in as safe a place as she could manage, so he could go after this goon who was attacking them in Houston's own home.

One way or another, the guy would pay for that, especially if that bullet had hit her.

Just the thought of that put Houston's heart in his throat. She could be hurt. She could be dying. And this SOB might be responsible.

He had to tamp down his rage and fear. He wouldn't be any good to them if he went after this guy with guns blazing.

Houston heard the movement in the far corner near a massive antique hutch, but he couldn't tell if Gabrielle had made the sound or if it'd come from their attacker. So he waited and tried to figure out exactly where she was. Each second seemed like an hour.

"Gabrielle?" he softly called out.

She didn't answer, but he heard the movement again.

Houston stayed positioned on the side of the archway, but he reached inside the room and grabbed a small onyx figurine from the table. He remembered something about it being extremely valuable, but right now its only value to him was that it could cause the distraction he needed.

Houston hurled it, not at the hutch where he'd heard the earlier movement, but at the center coffee table that was decorated with a glass bowl of crystal balls. The onyx piece slammed into all that glass, creating the loud noise that he'd hoped for.

He saw Gabrielle then. She darted out from the hutch and raced into the adjoining formal dining room.

Houston saw the gunman, too. He came up from behind the sofa and took aim at Gabrielle.

"Over here!" Houston shouted.

His shout worked, because the gunman swiveled in Houston's direction and fired. Houston fired, too, though he kept his shot low and aimed at the floor. He then turned and ran to the back of the foyer so he could try to intercept Gabrielle. If she continued to run through the maze of rooms, she'd eventually make it to the kitchen.

And so would the gunman.

There was no ideal place for a shootout in the house, but if Houston could just get to Gabrielle before the gunman did, he might be able to use the granite and stone counters to protect her from any bullets. Plus, once he had her semisafe, he could go after the gunman and take him off the face of the earth.

With his heart pounding a mile a minute, Houston hurried through the back of the house. He tried to keep his steps light so that he wouldn't give away his position, but it was nearly impossible, because his boots seemed to echo on the hardwood floors.

Thankfully, there were other echoes, too.

He heard the footsteps. Two sets, he thought. He prayed there were two, anyway, because that meant Gabrielle was still running. Still trying to escape.

Houston made it to the kitchen. It was empty, just as he'd expected, and the only illumination came from the milky light that was on over the wide, stainless steel stove. He hurried to the side of the room where Gabrielle should soon appear.

But the sound of the footsteps stopped.

Houston thought maybe his heart had stopped, too. Had she quit running because she was hurt and couldn't continue?

He wanted to call out to Gabrielle again, but he didn't want to let the gunman know he was in the kitchen waiting. Houston wanted the element of surprise on his hands. He knew every inch of this house, knew every nook and cranny.

Then he froze…and didn't like the sickening feel that formed in the pit of his stomach. Maybe the gunman was as familiar with the house, too, because the person behind that ski mask could be Dale. Or his father.

Hell.

Houston didn't want to have to kill either of them, but he would if one of them was the person responsible for this.

He waited again, but it didn't take long for him to hear

more movement. It seemed to come from both sides of the butler's pantry and overflow kitchen that the cooks used for canning and party preparations.

Unlike the formal sitting room, there weren't as many places to hide in there, but obviously Gabrielle and the gunman had found some spots.

Houston inched closer toward the room, and he tried to pick through the darkness and see if he could locate Gabrielle. Thanks to the moonlight filtering in through the windows, he finally saw her. She was stooped down at the side of a large, stainless steel prep table.

The relief flooded through him. She was alive and didn't appear to be hurt.

Gabrielle saw him, too, and her gaze locked with his. Houston put his finger to his mouth in a stay-quiet gesture, and she nodded.

The sound to his left sent Houston pivoting in that direction, and he aimed his gun. The man was there, somewhere amid the china and storage hutches, but unlike Gabrielle, Houston couldn't see him. So he waited, hoping the guy would make a mistake and leave cover.

"Mr. Sadler?" someone shouted.

The unexpected sound jolted through Houston, and it took him a second to realize it hadn't come from the butler's pantry but from the back door of the kitchen.

"Mr. Sadler?" someone called out again.

Houston recognized the voice. It was one of the ranch hands, and he started to pound on the door.

"I heard a noise," the ranch hand said, his voice so loud that it drowned out everything else.

Gabrielle ducked down out of sight.

"Are you okay?" the ranch hand asked. "Because what I heard sounded like gunshots."

Houston silently cursed. He wished to hell the ranch hand had just called the sheriff, but he probably hadn't. That would soon change. Houston couldn't call out to him and give away his position, so the guy just kept knocking on the door and kept calling out Houston's name.

"The phones aren't working," the ranch hand said. "Should I go get someone?"

Houston still didn't answer, and the ranch hand continued to knock. Soon, very soon, the guy would give up and just go get the sheriff. He hoped.

There was a scurry of movement from the butler's pantry, but it merged with the sounds of the ranch hand's voice and his persistent knocking. Houston heard another sound. Did Gabrielle gasp?

It was definitely some kind of sound of distress, and Houston knew he had no choice but to leave cover.

With his gun raised and ready, he raced to the entry of the pantry room and looked around.

Hell. This was not how he wanted this to play out.

Chapter Sixteen

Gabrielle tried to call out to Houston, she tried to tell him to watch out, but the hand that went around her mouth cut off any warning she wanted to give.

Oh, God.

The gunman had her again.

With all the noise and shouts from outside the kitchen door, Gabrielle hadn't heard the gunman scurry toward her, not until it was too late. He'd grabbed her, positioning her in front of him again.

This time she intended to fight back.

It was a risk, but she reminded herself that the gunman hadn't killed her when he first took her. So he obviously wanted her for something. Ransom, maybe. Maybe to force Houston to cooperate in some way. That was perhaps what the note was about.

"I'll give you what you want now," Houston had told the gunman, after he read that note. "But Gabrielle doesn't leave. She stays here."

Gabrielle could only imagine why this man wanted to get her away from the house. Maybe it was because he thought that might be the easiest way to get a ransom. Or maybe because this wasn't a simple kidnapping.

God, did he intend to torture her first? She couldn't imagine what she'd done to anyone to make them want to do that to her.

Houston was there, barely hidden behind the door-jamb that separated the kitchen from the room she was in. He couldn't fire. He couldn't get to her without giving the gunman an easy shot at killing them, so she wanted to do something before Houston reacted. She didn't want him hurt or worse.

Gabrielle swung her arms and her body, trying to break free, but the gunman held on, and he snapped her hard against his body. She wanted to scream and claw that mask off his face. She wanted to hurt him just as he was hurting her, but she forced herself to pull back. To stay calm.

If she continued to struggle. It would only prompt Houston to come to her aid. He was probably fighting the urge to do something, anything, that would get them out of this situation.

The knocking on the back door stopped, and Gabrielle hoped the man was on the way to get the sheriff, or some kind of help from the other ranch hands. She definitely didn't want the gunman to be able to get her off the ranch.

She thought of Lucas and prayed he wasn't crying or upset. Yes, he was too young to have a clue what was going on, but he might pick up on Lily Rose's fear. Gabrielle had to do something fast so she could get back to her son and keep Houston out of the line of fire.

Despite the death grip the gunman had on her, Gabrielle continued to struggle. The gunman continued to hold on to her, and he jerked her backwards until they were against the wall, with his gun aimed not at her but at Houston.

"Don't!" Gabrielle shouted when Houston started to lunge forward.

She felt the gunman's hand tense until his muscles felt like iron, and she knew he would shoot. But why was he so willing to do that, if he intended Houston to pay some kind of ransom to get her back?

Houston stayed put, thank God. He didn't lower his gun. He kept it trained on the man holding her hostage.

"I have money in my office," Houston told him. "It's not as much as you're asking, but there's plenty of stuff around the house that you could take."

The man only shook his head and continued to point his weapon.

Houston moved, just slightly. He crouched down a fraction. "There's also a safe in my dad's office," Houston said, trying again, "and there's some jewelry. Why don't you let Gabrielle go, and I can give it all to you?"

She felt the man tense again, and she didn't think it was because he was about to shoot. Was Houston getting through to him at the mention of the safe in Mack's office? Or was his reaction because of something else?

Gabrielle hated the thought of giving this monster one cent, but she also didn't want him in the house—not around Lucas. And if money and jewelry would get him to leave, then it seemed a small price to pay.

The gunman started to move with her, dragging her with him as he inched toward the kitchen. Gabrielle struggled, trying to delay and trying to buy Houston and her some time so they could figure out what to do.

Basically, they only had two options: continue to bargain with him, or wait until he made a mistake.

The waiting was hard, but Gabrielle held on to the hope that the ranch hand had called for help. Of course, that might create a new, dangerous scenario, if the gunman felt trapped. He could possibly try to shoot his way out of there.

"Where are you taking her?" Houston asked.

Of course, the gunman didn't answer.

Houston shifted his position, moving back as the gunman and she moved closer. He ducked to the side of the fridge when the gunman maneuvered her into the kitchen.

She saw Houston's face then—his expression. Every muscle in his body was primed and ready for this fight, but she also saw the worry, too.

"It's okay," she tried to reassure him. Which was laughable considering she was literally being kidnapped while Houston had a gun trained on the man holding her.

Gabrielle glanced around the kitchen to see if there was anything she could grab and use as a weapon. It would be a risk, but at this point anything was a risk.

Everything was clean and unfortunately in its place. The knives were at the other end of the room, on the counter and stored in a wooden block. She wouldn't be able to reach the gleaming copper and stainless steel pots hanging from an oval baker's rack.

Then she spotted the trio of horseshoes that had been mounted on the wall next to the door. The horseshoes had been modified in a key rack, and there were several sets of keys dangling from them. If she could manage to get one of the sets off a hook, she might be able to use them to gouge her attacker.

Gabrielle waited, holding her breath, and she continued to put up a token resistance in hope that the gunman wouldn't get suspicious. Each step took her closer to both the keys and the door. If she failed, if she couldn't stop him from getting her outside, then this might all be over.

She gave Houston one last look, and tried to convey to him what she was doing. He lifted his left eyebrow, questioning her, and Gabrielle gave a slight nod, then reached for the keys.

In the same motion, she slammed her elbow into the gunman, connecting with his stomach. He staggered back, just an inch. But an inch was all she needed.

"Get down!" she yelled to Houston.

But she couldn't see if he had done just that. Gabrielle grabbed the keys, turned and went after the man behind her.

He had already regained his balance and lifted his gun to aim it at her. The shot blasted through the air.

Had she been shot?

She wasn't sure, but she fought back anyway, and continued her attack. So did the gunman. He latched on to Gabrielle's neck. She used her arm to try to keep the gun pointed away from her, and she used the keys to go for his eyes, the only exposed part of his face.

Another shot.

Her ears were already ringing, the deafening echoes pulsing so loud through her head that she couldn't hear, but she thought she heard Houston call out her name.

She certainly felt someone grab her, and it wasn't the

gunman, who had the weapon in his right hand, and his left hand was clamped around the front of her throat.

Gabrielle raked the keys across the gunman's face, but she missed his eyes. She cursed, thinking she'd failed, but then the metal grooves on one of the keys caught onto some threads in the ski mask. She gave it a fierce jerk, tearing and pulling. The mask gave way, the momentum jerking it away from the gunman's face.

Gabrielle heard herself gasp. And then she froze. Because she couldn't believe the man who was staring back at her.

HOUSTON TRIED TO PULL Gabrielle to safety. He tried to get between the gunman and her. Those two fired shots had taken decades off his life, and he still didn't know if she'd been injured.

She *had* to be all right.

Everything inside him was yelling for him to protect her and get her out of harm's way. In that moment, he didn't care who was on the other end of that gun. Hell, he didn't care if he got shot. He just knew he had to do everything to save her.

He couldn't lose Gabrielle.

Another shot tore through the kitchen, and it ricocheted off something metal. Houston heard the deadly pinging sound, and once again tried to drag Gabrielle to safety.

The gunman held on to her throat while he waved the gun around. He was obviously trying to re-aim, to get off a kill shot, so Houston grabbed on to the man's right wrist. At that same moment, the man turned.

And Houston looked right into Jay Markham's face.

Part of him was relieved that it wasn't his father or Dale, but that didn't lessen the danger. Jay was obviously a man on a mission, and that mission appeared to be to kill his own sister.

The note Jay had given him asked for a five-million-dollar ransom for both Gabrielle and Lucas. Which meant Jay intended to kidnap them both. Gabrielle and Houston had apparently thwarted the part to include Lucas in on this, but Gabrielle was still right in the middle of the fray.

Someone knocked on the back door again. Houston didn't take the time to shout out to the person. He focused all his energy and attention on stopping Jay.

"I'll kill her!" Jay shouted. He slammed Gabrielle into Houston, and that jolt dislodged Houston's gun and sent it flying across the room.

Gabrielle went after her brother's face with the keys again, but Jay clamped harder on to her throat. Houston could tell she was having trouble breathing. At best, she might pass out, but Jay could also kill her with that deadly grip. He could crush her windpipe.

Houston had to do something fast.

He slammed Jay's hand against the wall, pinning the gun. But that didn't stop Jay from firing. This shot went into the ceiling, and Gabrielle gasped. Houston knew why.

Even though Lucas wasn't directly above the kitchen, he was just several rooms away, and that shot could have landed near him. Their baby could be hurt. The rage was instant, and Houston let it fuel him when he went after Jay. He turned Jay's gun, forcing it toward the floor. Jay pulled the trigger again.

The bullet slammed into the hardwood floor and

kicked up debris and splinters. Still, it was better than the alternative. A bullet in the floor meant it wasn't going anywhere near Lucas.

Houston moved Gabrielle out of the way so he could land his fist onto Jay's face. But the punch still didn't cause Jay to let go of Gabrielle throat. The man had to be working on pure adrenaline, because he seemed to have the strength of a dozen men.

Gabrielle made a horrible gasping sound that tore at Houston's heart. Jay seemed immune to Houston's punches to his face. He seemed oblivious to everything— except trying to choke his sister to death.

Jay dropped his gun and went after her with both hands, trying to squeeze the life right out of her.

"You chose him over me," Jay taunted. "Bad idea, Gabrielle. Never choose water over blood."

Someone bashed against the back door, obviously trying to open it, but Houston continued to pound his fist against Jay.

Gabrielle went limp, her body sagging forward against her brother.

Was she dead? Houston was too afraid to even consider the possibility, and he wasn't giving up. She might need mouth-to-mouth resuscitation, and for that to happen, he had to get Jay off her.

Jay moved, dragging Gabrielle in front of him to stop Houston's punches. It was a risk, because Jay still had his hands clamped on her throat, but Houston latched on to Jay's throat. And he didn't just squeeze. He jammed his thumbs against the man's Adam's apple and dug in.

It didn't take long, though the seconds felt like an

eternity, before Jay released Gabrielle. She slid to the floor, lifeless, unmoving.

Houston pushed aside his fears that she might be dead, and he latched on to Jay. He slammed the man face-first against the wall. It wasn't hard to put some muscle behind the slams, because Houston had to end this as soon as possible so he could get to Gabrielle.

The back door finally gave way, and three armed ranch hands bolted inside. Houston saw them out of the corner of his eyes, but he was too deep in the fight to respond. He bashed Jay against the wall, again and again, until the man went limp. Houston then shoved him in the direction of the ranch hands, just in case Jay was still capable of trying to come after Gabrielle again.

"Hold him!" Houston ordered.

In that moment, he didn't care if Jay was dead or alive. He only cared about getting to Gabrielle and saving her.

Houston dropped to his knees and put his fingers to her neck to check for a pulse. He couldn't feel anything because every inch of his hand was pulsing from the fight.

"Gabrielle?" Houston gently tapped her face, trying to revive her. Her eyes were closed. She didn't move.

"Get an ambulance," he told the ranch hands. Maybe, just maybe, they could get the phones to work. Because they would need a miracle.

Houston tilted back Gabrielle's head, lifted her chin and put his mouth to hers. He blew his own breath into her body and prayed that it would be enough to save her.

Chapter Seventeen

"I love you," Gabrielle heard someone say.

The voice seemed to come from far away, as if it were part of a dream. Or a nightmare.

She shook her head, trying to clear it of the jumble of sounds and images that were firing through her mind. Images of her brother trying to kill her.

Had Jay been the one to say "I love you"?

That didn't seem right, especially since it wasn't Jay's voice. It was Houston's.

She opened her eyes and saw his worried face…his *handsome,* worried face, she mentally corrected. He had his hand against her cheek and was staring at her as if he had expected the worst.

So had she. Gabrielle had thought that he might have been hurt, that Jay might have succeeded in whatever it was he had attempted to do in the kitchen.

She glanced around and realized she was no longer on the kitchen floor but in a bed. Houston's bed.

"The doctor's on the way," Houston told her.

Gabrielle listened, and she did indeed hear the sounds of a siren. An ambulance, no doubt.

And then Houston kissed her. It wasn't a soft, gentle

peck. It was filled with emotion, including some relief and more desperation.

Gabrielle didn't think she needed a doctor. True, she had lost consciousness, but everything seemed to be working, including the pain around her throat where Jay had choked her until she passed out.

"Lucas?" she said, trying to get up from the bed.

Houston put her right back down on the bed and pointed to the door. There stood Lily Rose, and she had a sleeping Lucas cradled in her arms. The nanny hurried across the room toward Gabrielle.

"The baby's fine," Lily Rose promised. But the woman looked worried when she stared at Gabrielle. "You will be, too, right?"

"Of course. I already am," Gabrielle told her. She caught on to Lily Rose's arm and eased her closer so she could kiss Lucas. The baby shifted, arching his back, and the corner of his mouth lifted in a smile.

Gabrielle smiled, too. If her son and Houston were safe, then everything was indeed all right.

Well, maybe.

"My brother?" she questioned, looking at Houston.

He shook his head. "The sheriff has him downstairs. He'll be arrested for attempted kidnapping and murder."

"He did it for money," she mumbled. That cut her to the bone.

"And because he was upset that you were here at the ranch." Houston took a deep breath and glanced at Lily Rose.

Houston didn't specifically ask the woman to leave,

but Lily Rose must have picked up on the nonverbal cue. "I should probably put Lucas to bed."

"No," Gabrielle insisted. "Leave him here with us. I don't want him out of my sight right now."

Lily Rose looked at Houston to make sure that was okay, and he nodded. The nanny gently placed the baby on the bed next to Gabrielle.

"I'll be next door," Lily Rose said, in a whisper. "Just call if you need me."

Gabrielle hoped that wouldn't be necessary. She was counting on a quiet, peaceful end to what had been a hellish night. First though, she needed to hear what Houston was apparently waiting to tell her.

"My brother?" Gabrielle prompted.

"I don't know all the details just yet, but Mack called a few minutes ago. Jay had sent ransom notes to both Dale and my father before he broke into the house."

That took a moment to sink it. "But how did he break in without tripping the perimeter alarms like Cordell did?"

"He literally walked up the driveway that leads from the road. There aren't any security alarms to trip on the driveway."

So Jay had taken the simplest approach, and at night there obviously hadn't been anyone about to notice him. Plus, he would have known about the location of the alarms, since he used to work at the ranch.

"Jay used a jamming device," Houston continued. "It wasn't sophisticated. Something he could have bought from any one of a dozen stores in San Antonio. But it did the trick. It prevented us from making a nine-one-one call."

It had, and it also showed premeditation. "So he didn't plan to kill me?" Gabrielle tried to brace herself, in case she was wrong.

Houston glanced away and huffed. "The ransom was for Lucas. He'd planned to take the baby. But when he didn't immediately find him, he took you instead. I think he was so angry with you that he snapped."

Yes, he had. She'd stared into her attacker's eyes, and she hadn't recognized her brother in that monster who wanted her dead.

"It's over now," Houston promised. "Jay will be locked away for the rest of his life, and he won't be able to hurt Lucas or you ever again."

She nodded, and winced at the pain in her throat. Still, she didn't want that pain to stop the conversation. Gabrielle had so many questions, including those first words she'd heard when she regained consciousness.

"I love you."

Had she imagined those words?

"Jay shot himself in the arm before he came to the ranch earlier," Houston went on. "He confessed to that. I didn't listen to everything he was saying—I wanted to get you off the floor and onto the bed. But he said something about giving himself a superficial wound so he could try to lure you into going with him." Because he wanted money. Or maybe his plan had been to kill her, even then.

"It doesn't appear that my father and Dale had anything to do with this," Houston continued. "We think Jay was acting alone."

She thought back through all the horrible events of the past two days. "Even in the car crashes?"

"Yeah." He paused, took a breath. "He could have just been trying to scare us."

Or Jay could have been trying to kill them because he'd thought she had chosen Houston over him. Jay's rage had ruled his senses, so he could have had murder on his mind. After all, if she were dead, Jay might have believed he could get the money from her life insurance.

"But just in case Jay had an accomplice or someone else was involved," Houston explained, "the sheriff will investigate everything, including what went on at the Cryogen Clinic."

That was good. An investigation would rid Houston of any lingering doubts and Dale and Mack's guilt. But Gabrielle had no such doubts anymore. She knew Jay had acted alone. If the others had coerced him in some way, Jay would have given them up immediately. He would have tried to put the blame on anyone but himself. She knew that now.

Maybe she'd always known it, and it had taken this near tragedy to make her truly understand that she wasn't her brother's keeper.

"One of the deputies arrested Cordell for trespassing," Houston continued. "I'll make sure he understands he won't be getting what Jay owes him from you. Also, the SAPD will take him into custody. They've already arrested his former henchman, and the guy is willing to take a deal to testify against Cordell for his part in the maternity hostage situation."

Good. She didn't want a man like Cordell resurfacing later. Gabrielle wanted her past behind her.

She reached up and touched Houston's face to get his

attention. "I don't want this to come between your father and you. Call him. Tell him that what's past is past. And also tell him that he'd better not try to manipulate me again."

Houston gave her a thin smile that didn't make it to his eyes. "You're generous." He gave Lucas a gentle stroke on his arm when the baby squirmed.

"Reasonable," she corrected. "He's your father. Dale's your friend and foreman. I think all of us could stand a fresh start, don't you agree?"

Gabrielle thought maybe he did, because Houston kissed her again.

The sirens stopped, and the red, swirling lights from the ambulance pulsed through the bedroom window. It wouldn't be long before the doctor arrived, and he would almost certainly want to take her to the hospital. She'd fight it. But in the end, Houston would win, and she would go to the hospital in the hopes of erasing some of that worry she still saw on his face.

Gabrielle wasn't sure how to say this, so she just asked, "Did you tell me you loved me?"

Houston blinked, then shrugged. "Yeah. I just thought I'd go ahead and get it out of the way."

Because her mind was still a little fuzzy, it took her a moment to work through that. "But you *do* love me?"

His gaze came to hers. "Absolutely. And it doesn't have a damn thing to do with the reasonable solution stuff I said earlier."

Gabrielle nearly melted at the "absolutely" part. The rest was just icing.

She heard the footsteps on the stairs. Medics, no

doubt. But she grabbed Houston and pulled him to her for a kiss. "Good," she said against his mouth. "Because I'm in love with you, too."

When she pulled back from the kiss, they were both smiling.

The medics, three of them, stormed into the room, but Houston held up his hand. "Give us just one minute," he said.

And much to her surprise, the medics stopped. What they didn't do was leave. They stood there, gear in hands, waiting to whisk her away.

Houston leaned in, his mouth hovering over hers. He had his left hand cradled around Lucas, and his right hand was on her arm. Cradling her, too.

"Marry me," Houston said. He didn't speak it softly, either, and the medics must have heard him, because they started to whisper.

Lucas stirred, too, and his eyes opened. He looked at her, almost as if he were waiting for her answer. Houston was definitely waiting.

"No reasonable solution," he repeated, perhaps because he thought he had to convince her. "I want the real thing. A marriage, a family, a home. And I want all those things with you, Gabrielle."

But Gabrielle didn't need convincing. There had been only three things in her life that she'd been absolutely positive about. One had been giving birth to Lucas. The other was the answer she wanted to give Houston.

"Yes," she told him. "I'll marry you."

That time the smile made it to his eyes. And his kiss. It was the kiss of a newly engaged man who was ready to get on with his life.

Gabrielle was ready for that, too.

And the third thing she was absolutely positive about was that this was what she wanted forever.

* * * * *

Don't miss the continuation of
Delores Fossen's miniseries
TEXAS MATERNITY: HOSTAGES
later in 2010!

 **HARLEQUIN®**

 **INTRIGUE®**

COMING NEXT MONTH

Available August 10, 2010

#1221 WANTED: BODYGUARD
Bodyguard of the Month
Carla Cassidy

#1222 COLBY VELOCITY
Colby Agency: Merger
Debra Webb

#1223 LOCK, STOCK AND SECRET BABY
Special Delivery Babies
Cassie Miles

#1224 ONE TOUGH MARINE
Cooper Justice
Paula Graves

#1225 ALPHA WARRIOR
Long Mountain Heroes
Aimée Thurlo

#1226 BUNDLE OF TROUBLE
Elle James

LARGER-PRINT BOOKS!

GET 2 FREE LARGER-PRINT NOVELS

PLUS 2 FREE GIFTS!

◆ HARLEQUIN®

INTRIGUE®

Breathtaking Romantic Suspense

HARLEQUIN®

A Romance

FOR EVERY MOOD™

Spotlight on
— Heart & Home —

Heartwarming romances
where love can happen
right when you least expect it.

See the next page to enjoy a sneak peek
from Harlequin® American Romance®,
a Heart and Home series.

*Five hunky Texas single fathers—five stories from
Cathy Gillen Thacker's* LONE STAR DADS *miniseries.
Here's an excerpt from the latest, THE MOMMY PROPOSAL
from Harlequin American Romance.*

"I hear you work miracles," Nate Hutchinson drawled. Brooke Mitchell had just stepped into his lavishly appointed office in downtown Fort Worth, Texas.

"Sometimes, I do." Brooke smiled and took the sexy financier's hand in hers, shook it briefly.

"Good." Nate looked her straight in the eye. "Because I'm in need of a home makeover—fast. The son of an old friend is coming to live with me."

She was still tingling from the feel of his warm palm. "Temporarily or permanently?"

"If all goes according to plan, I'll adopt Landry by summer's end."

Brooke had heard the founder of Nate Hutchinson Financial Services was eligible, wealthy and generous to a fault. She hadn't known he was in the market for a family, but she supposed she shouldn't be surprised. But Brooke had figured a man as successful and handsome as Nate would want one the old-fashioned way. *Not that this was any of her business…*

"So what's the child like?" she asked crisply, trying not to think how the marine-blue of Nate's dress shirt deepened the hue of his eyes.

"I don't know." Nate took a seat behind his massive antique mahogany desk. He relaxed against the smooth leather of the chair. "I've never met him."

"Yet you've invited this kid to live with you permanently?"

"It's complicated. But I'm sure it's going to be fine."

Obviously Nate Hutchinson knew as little about teenage

HAREXP0810

boys as he did about decorating. But that wasn't her problem. Finding a way to do the assignment without getting the least bit emotionally involved was.

Find out how a young boy brings Nate and Brooke together in THE MOMMY PROPOSAL, coming August 2010 from Harlequin American Romance.

MYSTERY MCF CASE FILES

LOOK FOR THIS NEW AND INTRIGUING

BLACKPOOL MYSTERY

SERIES
LAUNCHING AUGUST 2010!

Follow a married couple, two amateur
detectives who are keen to pursue
clever killers who think they have
gotten away with everything!

| Available August 2010 | Available November 2010 | Available February 2011 | Available May 2011 |